The Penny Portrait

Glynis Smy

Glynis Smy
The Penny Portrait

Copyright © 2014 Glynis J Smy
First Edition

All rights reserved in all media. No part of this book may be reproduced or transmitted in any form by any means, electronic or mechanical (including but not limited to the Internet, photocopying, recording or by any information storage and retrieval system), without prior written permission from the author and/or publisher.

The only exception is brief quotations in printed reviews.

ISBN-13: 9781503163720
ISBN-10: 1503163725

This is a work of fiction.
Names and characters are the product of the author's imagination and any resemblance to actual persons, living or dead, is entirely coincidental. Actual place/street names have been used, but not necessarily in the correct map area or town.
The author claims artistic licence.

Through Artistic Eyes

Moss green changing hue,
Rustic ochre against
Turquoise azure.
Magenta touches fuchsia,
Golden honey with hazel,
Ivy straddles terracotta.
Orange orbs drop
alongside lemon,
Peach strokes apricot,
Damson- cassis drapes
tendrils of jade.
The world is an artist's palette.

Copyright © Glynis Smy 2012

CHAPTER 1

A Misunderstanding

'No!' Elle screamed,' it should not be like this.' She pushed the man from her body and he slid ungraciously from the bed. He tried to snatch at the bedclothes but missed. The floundering moves he made as he fell back onto the floor would, under normal circumstances, be classed as rather comical. However, Elle sensed he was not amused. Before she had chance to try and make light of the matter, he had gathered his wits and gently pushed her back onto the bed.

'What do you think you are doing? You are sent to please not tease. Now lie down like a good girl and let me enjoy you'.

Elle struggled to sit upright but he had a heavy build. The more she wiggled and writhed, the more he took it as a sign she was a willing victim to his lusty desires. Frustration fought frustration, and Elle made one last push for freedom. Once she freed herself Elle stood beside the bed. She straightened the thin cotton gown she wore, and pulled her lank honey-gold hair from her face.

'Sir, I am sorry, so sorry. I am not teasing you, but I do need to leave. Sadly I fear a misunderstanding.' She lowered her head, and hoped the giant of a man would note her innocence. His voice had an authoritative tone with a distinctive sound of upper-class breeding. His voice also had a softness, and despite his size she could tell he was a gentle character. Not once had he been rough with her. Guilt made her falter but deep down she knew she could never lay with this man. She had been brought to the room by a valet, not fully understanding what was wanted from her, and at no point did she think this would be the outcome, it had crossed her mind she might have to clean a room but never to be entertainment for a gentleman.

Her sixteen years of innocence, living in a quiet village, had never encountered such a situation. She was indeed in a desperate state but not desperate enough to share her body.

Prior to his waking, she sat watching him sleep, and her artistic inner-being could not resist etching him. Her greatest joy was to sit with charcoal and draw. She captured his likeness well, and opted to tuck the drawing in her pocket, in her opinion it was too good to throw onto the coals burning in the grate. She scribbled, *The Man in Room Eighteen*, in the right-hand, bottom corner. It would be put into her box of drawings when she returned home. A quick glance at his clothing laid over the ornate rosewood chair, told Elle he was a man of means and like many, followed the fashion of Prince Albert, Queen Victoria's consort. The chances of him ignoring a shabbily dressed girl in her sixteenth year were minimal. Most people with money overruled the working class.

Think, Elle. Think!

Elle stared at the thick, plush carpet; blood red; crimson. An idea flashed through her frantic brain; one that might just save her from the awkward and frightening situation in which she found herself. She clutched at her lower belly and groaned.

The man sat up and stared at her. 'What's the matter with you? Are you sick?'

'No sir, I am in pain. I suffer from my monthly curse, I …'

The plan worked, the man jumped from the bed. As Elle was well aware, the highly improper conversation topic proved an embarrassment to him. The man hastily draped the sheet around his body, no longer emboldened in manly needs, he showed himself flaccid, and irritated. A shiver of fear triggered a sense of survival in Elle, and she realised the need to act swiftly, despite her gut instinct telling her the man would do her no harm. There was something about him, a kind aura, yet Elle decided not to take any chances.

She screwed up her nose to indicate more pain. 'I am afraid I would be unclean for you to bed me, sir.'

He shook his head.

'Damn you women and your monthly excuses.' He moved towards her and towered over her. Nervous, Elle, sure the fear inside must shine through her eyes, remained in humbled status.

Please do not let him see my fear. Do not give him power over me.

He tilted her chin upwards. 'Pity. I would have enjoyed you. Pretty thing. Come back to me when you are next free. I will make it worth your while. Here, take this, you look in need.' He handed her a coin. 'Find our mutual friend, and inform him to send another to take your place.' The man flopped onto the bed and folded his arms behind his head. She had been dismissed. With relief Elle let herself out of the room and into the corridor, she ran the full length and down one flight of stairs. The coin, hot in her hands as she gripped tight, was too precious to lose. It had become her lifeline. As was a small charcoal drawing. Both items were her only possessions. She tucked the coin into her pocket alongside the picture.

At the bottom of the stairs she stopped to take in her surroundings. Ahead, by the door that led out onto the main street, stood a man in a uniform. Another man in a smart, gold braided suit stood behind a large desk.

Elle panicked. This area did not appear familiar at all. She could not remember coming through such a plush entrance. She moved behind a large planter with a vast amount of greenery overhanging and watched people mill around the luxurious reception area. Elle was in awe of the clothing worn by obvious members of the gentry. Jewellery adorned the necks of young and old women.

When the valet had sneaked her upstairs the place had been silent. She shifted from foot to foot. Nature added to the urgency of the moment.

'What are you doing behind there? Get out this instant.'

A large hand and deep voice startled Elle. She looked up to see a grim face smothered with whiskers staring down at her.

'I um-I'

'Get out from behind the plant and remove yourself from the building. This place is not for the likes of you. Now clear off.' The concierge pulled her to her feet and pointed towards the back exit. 'Out.'

Elle didn't need to be told twice but not wishing to bump into the man from the night before in fear he might have other guests to entertain, she ran for the main doors. She brushed past silk gowns and inhaled wafts of rose water perfume. She sensed their contemptuous eyes on the back of her neck as she headed out through large glass doors edged in gold. An atmosphere of combined forces willed her to leave their sumptuous surroundings and Elle had no desire to stay. They outclassed her tenfold.

Terrified, she ran for several streets before the need to rest her lungs and empty her bladder became imperative. She leaned against a wall and took stock of her situation. She craved sleep, and needed somewhere to rest for the night but was reluctant to use her precious coin to pay for a bed.

Exhaustion took over and she slipped behind a large building. Several doors led out onto the dark alley she found herself in, and Elle glanced around for a corner to relieve herself. Her body was short of energy and she needed a place to rest. Smells and a warm glow from lights from one doorway tempted her over to investigate further. Beside the door stood two large containers and Elle slid between them. She tugged her shawl around her shoulders and curled into a ball. Tiredness washed over her, her body, pushed to its limits, trembled.

Elle had spent days walking. Her only release came when she had been approached by the valet at the hotel she passed by several hours ago. Confused by his intentions but in need of sustenance, Elle had allowed herself to be drawn into his suggestion. She was to entertain a gentleman in room eighteen, in exchange she would be given hot milk, and the man himself would pay her a coin. On arrival to his room the valet had motioned to the sleeping man in the large four poster bed.

'When he awakes he will have need of you. "Wash over there and be quiet', were the only instructions given.

While Elle waited she was drawn to the features of the sleeping mound. Large plump lips, coal-black hair with a wisp of grey here and there, and long dark eyelashes; all attractive and indicative of a well groomed male. His olive skin and even-arched eyebrows made his features a pleasure to look at, and his shaven chin looked soft enough for Elle to want to reach out and touch him. Instead she broke off a piece of charcoal from the fire place and found a scrap of paper in a nearby waste basket. She spent forty-five minutes frantically sketching the image before her. Elle, too scared to leave, and not so innocent of what lay before her, did not wish this moment to be tainted in any way. She had seen men and women fornicate in alleyways and questioned her mother as to what was their purpose. Her mother informed her it was not a game to play, and warned her of the consequences of such activity.

She accompanied the conversation with a swipe of her hand across Elle's head to ensure the message stayed with her.

The ticking clock, the crackle of the fire and the gentle snores of a handsome man made new memories for Elle. The whole scene mesmerised her and her natural instinct captured the peaceful innocence in the only way she knew how; by using her talent. Elle often used drawing as a way to release fear or joy when words failed her. Her parents had not encouraged her gift and lack of money meant Elle went without the paper supplies she secretly desired. Her dream to own paints and canvas were just that; a dream. Even more nowadays.

'Please let it be warmer tonight'.

Elle whispered to the night sky as it took over from the twilight. She pulled her legs to her chest and huddled down for sleep. Her stomach growled. She had eaten nothing for two days. One glass of milk and a sweetmeat taken from a plate in the hotel room, are all that had passed her lips.

Tomorrow I will eat. Tomorrow I will return home.

CHAPTER 2

Heading home

The following morning rain drizzled down on Elle, the sky as grey as her mood. Rats disturbed her during the night and hunger gnawed at her insides. She stretched out the aches in her limbs and leaned against the wall to regain her balance. White flakes floated in front of her eyes and giddiness took over. Blackness followed as she lost control of her body and slumped to the floor.

***

'What's this, a mangy stray dog for the pot, Bill?' A gruff male voice accompanied a floating sensation as Elle came around from her faint.

'No. Some scrap of a girl I found by the bins. Fetch a blanket from the back room for me.' Another deep voice reached her ears; a softer, more caring tone.

'Old Burgess finds her there will be hell to play. You are too soft for your own good.' The gruff voice grumbled on, becoming fainter as the man moved out of the room.

Elle tried to move.

'Stay still, there's a girl. My old back is groaning. Hurry with that blanket, Jack. My back is nigh on killing me. There. By the fire. Quick, warm some milk. Stop staring at me like I have lost my mind. Move man.'

Elle felt herself being lowered into a chair and a warmth surrounded her. Her eyelids refused to lift. She so wanted to see face behind the kind voice.

'Here lass. Drink this. Not too fast or you'll throw it back. Well done. Slowly.'

The rim of a warm mug touched her lips and she supped at the honeyed milk.

'There. Well done. All finished. Good girl. Now get some rest while I fetch you a slice and bread.'

'A slice and bread? Are you crazy man? Burgess will have you out of here with one flick of his wrist.' The gravelled voice of the other man in the room vibrated Elle's ears but still she was too weak to move.

'Hush your mouth. Burgess is in Chelmsford with his missus today. Besides, I shall use my allowance, I will eat less supper. Now get on with the shoe shine and take them up to Major Sharp. You know he hates waiting. Leave me to do what I want. If she were my girl I would want someone to do the same.' Elle noted the voice soften with a hint of sadness.

'Ah. Now we come to the nub of the matter. Your girl runs away and you take in strays. Let's hope your girl is as lucky as this whippersnapper. Her arms are so thin, they will break with one movement. Bonny though. Pretty when cleaned up, I'll wager.' The voice disappeared out of the room and pots and pans clattered in the background. A clock ticked and gradually the aroma of bacon filled the room. Her mouth watered and saliva trickled from the corners of her mouth. What she wouldn't give for a slice.

'Well now. Can you manage to sit up?' A tug at her sleeve startled Elle, and she realised she was being addressed. She gave a weak nod of her head and slowly opened her eyes.

A pair of kind twinkling faded with age, blue ones stared back into hers. Creases around them indicated the man was smiling. She attempted to wiggle upright in the large horsehair seat. Stray wisps of rough hair scratched at her legs as she moved. The room began to spin and she inhaled deeply.

'That's it. Nice and steady. Old Bill has time to wait. Mind the bread and slice might get cold. Fried in dripping and dipped in egg for you, little one. Come on get some down you. Do you good.'

Elle couldn't believe her ears. So much kindness from one human being. She reached out for the plate where her prize sat waiting to be devoured. The first bite was chewed and swallowed with such haste she nearly choked. Bill sat down beside her and offered her the mug at regular intervals. Each mouthful was washed down with more milk. She wiped the plate clean with the last piece of crust.

'Thank you.' The words came out as a whisper. Elle wiggled further up the chair and enjoyed the fullness of her belly. A belch escaped her lips and she put her hand to her mouth. Embarrassed she glanced at the man. His large whiskered mouth curved upwards and he gave a loud guffaw of a laugh.

'There's all the thanks I need. A satisfied stomach.' He pulled the blanket up to her chin. 'I can't keep you here indefinitely. Get some sleep for an hour and I will wake you when my chores are finished. We will talk more after.'

'Thank you.' Elle muttered again. Within seconds the noises of the kitchen disappeared.

'Time to wake up. Come on sleepyhead. Wakey-wakey. We need to sort out your situation.' Bill's voice interrupted her sleep.

The warmth of the room was such a comfort but she knew it was time for her to leave.

'Where you from?' Bill was munching on a large slice of bread as he spoke. Elle felt guilty as she had heard him mention he had given up his share of food for her.

'Parkeston village, sir.' She ventured.

'Parkeston? As in near Dovercourt? How come you are here? It is a fair few miles from Colchester.' Bill continued to chew on his meal.

Elle nodded. 'Yes, indeed, a long way but I need to find my parents.'

'Ah. Parents eh? Are they in town, where they staying? I will get you back to them.' Bill stood up and placed his dishes in a large sink. Elle scrambled out of the chair and shivered as the blanket fell away. The least she could do was help him with the clearing of the plates.

'I could not find them. They mentioned they were seeking work and returning within two days. That was three weeks past. I came to search for them four days ago. I looked in all the obvious places. The big halls are where they usually find temporary work in the winter months. I have to confess I cannot find them.' A large tear dripped off the end of her nose and she wiped it away with the back of her hand. 'I made up my mind to head back home. Just in case they returned. Mother will be frantic with worry if I am not there. It was foolish of me to come. The landlord wants his rent you see, and I don't have any money. He is not a pleasant man, and I am afeared of what he might do if the money is not available upon his next visit.' Elle remembered the coin in her pocket. She felt for it and was relieved to feel the cool metal beneath her fingers. Then a thought crossed her mind.

Should I offer it for my food? I have money to pay, after all. It is not enough for the rent. Food, I will pay for the food.

Slowly she pulled the precious penny from her pocket and held between her fingers. With a slight hesitation, yet feeling guilty at the reluctance to let go, she offered up the coin to Bill.

'I do have a penny. I can pay for my meal. It is not enough to satisfy the landlord, but it will pay for my supper. Of which, I am most grateful.'

Bill knelt before her, she heard his knees click as he did so, she winced.

'Keep your money. Use it to get yourself home. Chances are your parents will be waiting to greet you.'

Elle put her coin back into her pocket, and her fingers touched the drawing she etched the day before. Remembering the situation her cheeks flamed hot. Suddenly an idea hit her.

'Do you have paper sir?'

'Paper? What sort of paper?' Bill creased his brow in question.

'Something that can be drawn on. Just a small piece will do.' Elle glanced around the room. Frantically looking for something that would be suitable. She did not want to lose the opportunity of giving something back to Bill for his kindness.

'Here's a rough piece that was tied around a batch of papers for Mr Burgess. Will that do you? What are you up to?'

'You'll see.' Elle chirruped with excitement. The food lifted her spirits and gave her renewed energy. 'Please sit over there. Yes. On the stool by the pots.'

Bill did as she asked and Elle fashioned a piece of charcoal from the fireplace with a small sharp knife. She held up her hand when he moved. She noted the bemused look upon his face.

'Sit still ... if you please. I can draw. I shall draw you, you'll see.' She muttered while her tongue poked out between her teeth. Bill eventually became the ideal subject and sat with a grin on his face.

Within twenty minutes Elle finished her sketch. Pleased with the outcome, she signed her initials in one corner and shyly handed it to a bemused Bill.

'Glory. Would you look at that? It is like looking in a mirror. What a gift your fingers have. An eye for the image that is for sure. Here, Jack. Take a look at this.' Bill handed over his picture to the man who walked into the room. Elle knew his face would not be one she would enjoy drawing. Pot marked, pale and uninteresting would be how she would describe it if asked. He had cruel eyes, and made her most uncomfortable in his presence.

'She certainly has captured you well, Bill. A fine likeness. You are a clever thing.' He ruffled Elle's hair. His bony fingers scraped her scalp. She did not feel easy with this man as she did with the one who had most probably saved her life.

'I will treasure it always. In fact wait a minute.' Bill moved to a large cupboard area and returned with a small frame. It was tarnished but served the purpose he desired.

'This lot is for the scrap cart. The missus upstairs is getting rid of it all. I am sure she won't begrudge me keeping this back. It is perfect for the job. I will treasure it always. Thank you...er...E.B?'

It occurred to Elle she had not been asked nor given her name and noted Bill had realised the same.

'Elle. Elle Buchanan.' She said.

'Thank you, Elle Buchanan. It is a fine picture. Reward indeed.' Bill placed the frame on the table. Elle was thrilled to see he took pleasure in it and even more so to see her work in a frame.

'Do not give up on that gift of yours. It will be the making of you. You have a talent many would desire.'

'She most certainly has, she has captured your ugly mug on a good day that's for sure.' Jack laughed. All three joined in with the joke and for the first time for many weeks, Elle smiled.

'I must go now. I need to return home before dark and have miles to travel. I do thank you for your kindness and will visit you again one day.' She pulled her shawl around her shoulders. It was time to leave before she became too comfortable.

'Do take care. Sorry I don't have the coins to help you on your way.' A sadness crossed Bill's face.

'You have given me more than enough, thank you. I will be fine. I have my penny and a full belly. Thank you, both.' Elle looked at the two men before her. One a giant of a man with large hands and a wide smile. The other, skinny and sly looking. Something inside told her he was not to be trusted and she would be wise to move away from his environment.

'It has been our pleasure.' Bill replied. 'Can I be rude and ask your age?'

Elle looked at him. Surprised by his question.

'I have six years and ten, sir. I turned so this past October. All Hallows Eve to be precise. Why do you ask?'

Bill sighed. 'I thought so. The same age as my Aggie. You are alike. Both have the same corn coloured hair, except she doesn't have blue eyes. Brown. Hers are brown. Two years since I saw her last. Ran away with a soldier with a glib tongue. Still that is history, and now is now. You get yourself back home and enjoy the love of your parents. Go. Shoo. I have work to do.'

Elle moved to him and embraced his wide girth. She laid her head against his chest. No words could explain what this man had done for her in such a short space of time. He had given her food and hope.

'Goodbye Bill.'

She pulled the large door to the outside world open and stepped outside. The grey drizzle was still falling, and it was a reluctant Elle who stepped out into the puddles and made her way to the main streets.

Her damp hair clung to her cheeks, she wished she could remove them, but her hands were busy clutching hold of her shawl the wind pulled at so intently. Elle put up with the discomfort for the sake of what little warmth she could muster. The winds grew in strength, and Colchester Town gave an unfriendly farewell to the young girl as she moved away from its boundaries.

Offered several short rides on the carts and wagons that wove the streets of the various villages she passed through, Elle accepted each one. The last driver left her on the edge of Bradfield, there appeared to be no other travellers heading her way and Elle had no choice but to trudge along on foot. Sore feet in inadequate shoes. She made her way past the church keeping the view of the river Stour to her left. She ignored temptation to rest under the eaves of the vestry, and continued walking at a steady pace. She knew the waters flowed towards home and she would not get lost if she followed this route. At each mound circled by trees she crossed herself. A habit formed from her mother's information of the plague victims and their burial grounds. Elle, always grateful for her humble life, ensured she sent out a small prayer for the dead who lay in the fields she worked or walked.

About a mile of trudging along with Bill and his bacon meal on her mind, she thought about her situation. She told Bill her mother would be frantic with worry if she were not home. It was a statement far from the truth. Her parents often whispered together, and a few times Elle had overheard them discussing money and burdens. She was mentioned as one of their largest burdens. They were not loving people, and often left her for long periods when they needed to work outside of the village. At times they forgot she needed feeding or fresh clothing, and when they did remember, they reminded her she held them back from finding work in the big houses, where they could live-in. No affection had ever been offered, and many times her father commented when she was of age they would find her a position elsewhere. Both of them drank excessive amounts of alcohol, and Elle often wondered if they stopped whether they might find better work for themselves.

Her Grandmother expressed the same sentiments, and mostly to their faces. Argument upon argument created a hostile atmosphere, and Elle's miserable life never altered from one day to the next. She told herself she must love them, they were her parents after all, and she was an ungrateful child if she did not. Today it occurred to her she was an unwanted child.

To her relief, the driver of a dray stopped and offered her a ride to the edge of Wrabness Woods. The back of the dray was empty, and he told her he headed her way in order to collect the copperas collected by his wife and children. Elle needed no second telling to lay herself down and get some rest. She rested on old sacks, and drifted in and out of sleep, her parents continually on her mind. Home was getting closer and she prayed her parents would be there to greet her.

When she first set off in search of her parents little did she realise how far she would travel. The cart driver who originally took her to Colchester, chatted so much Elle did not focus on her surroundings. The time passed swiftly as they journeyed to the town she was sure her parents had headed for in search of work. Unfortunately, the journey back was not so short, nor as comfortable.

Her feet ached, as did every bone in her body. On arrival at the woods she couldn't believe her luck when a carpenter offered her a lift to Ramsey village, less than three miles from her home. His cart was not so comfortable but Elle was grateful for the seat, nonetheless. The deep voice of the driver cut into the silence every now and then, and it jolted Elle back from her short naps. The man had been kind enough to stop and offer her relief from walking. Unfortunately she had little energy to enjoy an enthusiastic conversation.

'Nearly there. The sails of the windmill always brighten my day. I live close by and am always glad to see them turning. My father helped carve them. Waving to welcome me home.'

The man pointed towards four large wooden sails moving gracefully-almost lazily-round and around. Elle nodded and smiled.

Home. Welcome home. Home.

The smell of the fresh cut wood on the cart and the warmth of the sun rising from behind a cloud for the last hour of daylight, made all thoughts of doom disappear for a short moment.

'The sails are getting bigger and bigger. I can understand why you feel welcomed sir. You are right, they *are* waving to us.' Elle felt she should say something.

'I will drop you down by the bottom of the farmland. If I were not so busy I would take you onward to the village but sadly, I cannot lose the daylight.' The man clicked his tongue to urge his horse through a narrow gateway and into a dry lane.

'I am grateful to you sir. My parent's cottage is not too far away. I will be home within a short time.'

'Well now I don't feel quite so guilty. Nearby you say?' He jumped down from the cart and helped her clamber down. Elle had short legs and they dangled a few feet off the floor. 'Keep still and I will lift you down. You certainly won't break my back. Light as a feather, nothing of you. There.'

Feet planted firmly on the ground, Elle looked up at the man; he was tall with smiling eyes. She could not help but smile back.

'Thank you for your kindness, sir, and Godspeed. Yes, we live on Spike Island. Near the entrance to the lanes leading to Dovercourt.'

'Spike Island. Cinder City. Why you local folk call Parkeston by any other name than its own is beyond me.' He shook his head. Elle could not supply him with an answer and just shrugged her shoulders. She waved her goodbye and made her way along the last mile or so of her journey.

CHAPTER 3
Cold Greetings

Nothing could describe the depth of disappointment that swamped Elle as she walked towards the rundown cottage a few yards away. No welcome plume of smoke wove its way from the narrow chimney pot perched on the grey slate roof. Her parents were not home. She knew the first thing her mother would have done would be to light a fire if she had returned.

The wooden door had swollen in the damp weather and Elle struggled to push it open. A musty smell of cold and damp confirmed her fears. No one had been home since she left. A cockroach scuttled across the floor and in temper Elle stomped her foot on its back.

Where are you?

'Mother? Father?' She called out in hope. Silence replied.

She climbed the few stairs to the second floor of the small house. The door to her small box room was open and she knew what was inside. A few personal possessions and a rickety bed with worn, drab bedding. Her parent's room door was shut. As always, Elle tapped lightly. Not expecting a response, but again, she hoped for one.

Slowly she turned the handle. What she saw brought a loud scream to her throat but she swallowed it down. The bed made a bold statement in the room. There was no sign of the large stuffed mattress. Her parents clothing, normally draped over two chairs, had gone. Her mother's hairbrush was no longer on the small table between the chairs. Everything they owned, they had taken. Had Elle looked in the room days ago she would have saved herself from a long, tiring journey and found the truth earlier. Her parents had run away. They had left her; abandoned her.

Why have you deserted me?

Neither parent had a loving bone in their body, but they were her parents. They provided for her these sixteen years, and she never for one moment thought them capable of just leaving her penniless. Eventually the suppressed scream came forward as a raging roar of denial.

'NO! How could you? I am your child. How could you leave me like this?' Elle ran to her room and flung herself onto the bed. The thin blanket felt damp but Elle's tears added to that during the fifteen minutes she lay sobbing. Eventually, the cold air in the room became unbearable and Elle went back down to the large room that acted as kitchen and living quarters. It was a cheerless room at the best of times but today it was the worse place on earth as far as Elle was concerned. She pulled a few sticks from a heap by the hearth and prayed they would not take too long to light. The hazy autumn sun had dipped low and the light subsided. She looked around for the candle holder that normally sat on the top of the mantle but it was not there.

Everything. You have taken everything.

The fire flicked into life but gave little warmth. Elle knew she needed to find a larger log from the woodpile behind the house. It had been nearly depleted when she left for Colchester but was sure there was one decent sized off-cut left. She slipped around the back of the house and rolled the log to the door. Something caught her eye. Her father had not taken a shirt from the line that ran along the side of the house. She pulled it from its wooden pegs and put it on over her clothing. The sleeves dangled as she shoved the log along the floor. It took all her strength to lift it into the fireplace but was rewarded within minutes by a roaring spit as it took hold.

She pulled the shirt off and lay it on the back of a chair. It would serve as a night shirt and save her frock. The one and only garment she owned looked grubbier than its normal shade of grey, and Elle decided it was in need of a wash. She placed a large iron pot of water onto the log. She slipped off her gown and under garments and put them inside for a boil. She scooped them out after the water had heated, and its colour indicated all grime had been released. Wrung out she laid them on the back of the two chairs facing the fire and watched steam rise. They would be dry by morning, they were only thin. Not wanting to waste the hot water she found a large tin bowl and filled it carefully. She slipped off the shirt and washed down her body enjoying the warmth. She dipped in a glass jar and poured it over her hair. Squeezing her locks dry she replaced the shirt. Hauling the pot off the fire she poured it into the large bowl in the sink.

Thank goodness for the landlord. At least they didn't run away with his things.

She washed out the jar taking care not to burn her fingers. A tin plate that had housed a scrap of green soap got a good scrubbing, it would serve well enough for her to eat from-when she found something to eat.

Elle slipped outside and immediately regretted doing so. The cold night air had settled over the village and chilled her skin. She pumped the iron water pump with grim determination. Anger fuelled her muscles. She put down the pot and moved towards an area of garden that had once housed row upon row of vegetables. Four days ago a small cabbage sat in solitude and Elle prayed her parents had not lifted it from its bed. The moon was not bright but gave enough light to show her that supper was still there.

She pulled and tugged at leaves, just a few would stave off the hunger she was beginning to feel. In the morning she would scout around for more stray edibles. She knew there was a rosemary plant by the back door and broke off a stem before going back indoors. The fire had warmed the room and the damp smell had given way to an inviting smoked wood aroma.

A plate of cabbage leaves and a cup of rosemary tea warmed Elle's body, and she decided to drag her bedding downstairs. The thought of sleeping in her room tonight did not appeal. She moved the worn pine table alongside the wall and placed her thin mattress a few feet away from the fire but within view of its glow. The log was burning well and she hoped it would last throughout the darkened, cooler hours. Curling into a ball she snuggled down for the night.

***

'Open this door. Now. Open this door immediately.'

Confused, Elle scrambled to her feet. The frantic banging on the door and loud voice she recognised as the landlord's, startled her. She had just drifted into a light sleep when the noise became louder and louder.

'One moment. Wait one moment.' She called out while wrapping the thin blanket around her body for dignity sake.

She turned the large key in the door. It had always stayed in a drawer by the sink and Elle had never known it to be used. However tonight she felt in need of security and was thankful she had locked herself inside.

'It's a bloody cheek that's what it is.' The squat, bald figure strode into the room and stood with his hands on his hips.

'Mr. Stockwell. What is the matter? It's me Elle.'

The man turned and squinted at her. Then nodded his head furiously.

'I know exactly who you are young lady and it is a cheek you and your parents have, coming back here.'

Elle watched as he paced amongst the bed and table. His anger very much in evidence. He frightened her.

'I am sorry. I do not understand.'

'Three months I have not had a penny piece from your father for rent. Not one penny piece. All his pleading that he was going to get the money finally got my goat. Now he has the cheek to return and set up home again. After I warned him. Oh yes, I warned him. Get out and stay out. No money- no home. Where is he, Buchanan? Get down here. Buchanan.'

The man moved to the staircase.

'He is not here sir. My parents have left. It is only me here.'

'Only you? They coming back?' He peered into her face and Elle could smell the fumes of ale upon his breath. She needed to calm the man down and protect herself. Her mistake was giving away the fact she was alone.

'First thing in the morning. He said he had found work. I was to go back to the cottage and wait for his return. He will bring the rent owing in the morning. My mother has stepped out for a visit to Ray Farm, where they have found work. She will be back soon. Unfortunately she doesn't have your money. But father...' She hoped the lie would be forgiven, but Elle knew it was her only protection. Her mother had never felt comfortable in this man's company and had often warned Elle to steer clear of his lecherous hands.

'Tell your father I want that money no later than the hour of nine tomorrow morning. Tell him if he is a minute late he will regret playing me for a fool. I will be here in person. Remind him I have men who will carry out tasks of any kind for a coin. You tell him that. No games young lady. I can play too.' The leery grin he gave Elle sent shivers through her body. There was no denying what he meant.

He pushed past her and went to the door. Elle held her breath. For one dreadful moment she though he was going to say more.

'I will tell him, sir. Goodnight.'

She locked the door as soon as she heard his steps fade away. It was time to move quickly. Tomorrow she needed to be away from the cottage and the wrath of an irate landlord. When he realises he has been duped by a young girl he will not be a happy man.

Where shall I go? There is no one to turn to, no family. Think, Elle. Think.

Not wishing to waste time, she thought about her predicament while collecting a few items from around the room. To her annoyance she came across half a candle.

Where were you when I needed you?

She decided against using it and placed it with the plate and glass jar on the table.

Gathering her scrap of a sheet from the mattress she laid it out and placed the items in the centre. Her damp clothes remained by the fire. She would need to wear them in an hour or so and they needed to be much drier if she wanted to avoid a chill. She ran upstairs to her bedroom and tugged at a loose floorboard in one corner. It was dark but Elle knew every inch of her room, and what she was looking for,-her treasures- as she called them.

A few drawings, a pebble with a hole in the middle and a small cameo brooch her Grandmother had given her five years previous; one year before her death. Elle knew it had no monetary value but that wouldn't stop her father from trying to get a coin for it, so she had hidden it away. Out of sight-out of mind.

The pebble no longer held any affection in her heart. It was found by her mother and given to her for a birthday gift on her fifteenth birthday. Today it meant nothing. As much as she meant to her mother. She tossed it to one side.

The drawings were of the home, and surrounding area she was about to leave, and had happy memories. Elle knew they were good enough to earn her a few pennies if required.

All the time she had been preparing the contents of her makeshift carrier, Elle wracked her brains about where to head for in the morning. She had no desire to remain in Parkeston, but wanted to remain within the Ramsey or Dovercourt parish. Elle loved the seaside and would often walk for miles to sit and watch the tide ebb and flow. Her Grandmother taught her how to collect shellfish and edible seaweed during the summer months. She stayed with her Grandmother while her parents worked when she was too young to help but when her Gran died the pleasures of the shore lacked that something extra special.

With all her goods tied into the knotted carrier and her clothing drying by the fire, Elle curled once again upon the mattress. She needed to rest and make decisions. The warmth of the fire encouraged sleep and Elle gave up fighting her heavy eyelids. She estimated the time must be after ten and she intended to be out of the cottage once dawn arrived.

CHAPTER 4

Decisions

Elle stirred and stretched her body in cat-like fashion. The room chilled her body once again, no longer was there a welcome glow, the log burned out, and in its place lay whitened flakes of ash. Had she wanted to linger for a hot drink, Elle would have been out of luck.

A small ray of sunshine filtered through the grubby window reminding Elle it was time for her to leave. Sunrise. It was around seven-thirty and Elle wanted to put a good hour between her and the landlord. First she needed to search around for straggling vegetables in the garden. The sun deceived the world, and soon clouds cloaked out its rays. The first drops of rain brought with them a depressive air, and Elle hastily gathered more cabbage leaves and rosemary sprigs. No other vegetables were evident which posed a problem with regard to her food source. The penny had been spent on route home the day before so there were no funds for purchasing bread, or even flour to make a small loaf. Elle had no choice, she had to move closer to the only food source she knew; the beach. As she turned to go inside to fetch her belongings she spotted an old pull along trolley her father made for her when she was a little girl. He would sit her in it and pull her through the leafy lanes to purchase fish along the quayside of Harwich. Shaking off the memory, Elle cleared away the broken tools that lay on top and noted with glee that all four wheels were intact. Although a little rusty, with effort they turned. She rummaged through the broken metal of the discarded tools and found a snapped scythe tip. Elle unravelled a piece of twine from around an old axe handle and wound it around the sharp blade of the scythe tip. Although rustic and bordering on the dangerous side, Elle had made herself a crude knife. Now she could carry more items, she made no hesitation in hacking at the stem of the precious cabbage. It sat pride of place on the small trolley. Alongside it Elle placed the handles and metal scraps of the old tools. Not really sure what she would do with them she was satisfied they might come in useful. Feeling no guilt about taking from the landlord, she loaded the cooking pot and rolled up thin mattress. Her needs were greater than his. November was making way for December and she would need warm food and something to lie upon. Without the cook pot and mattress it would be impossible to keep warm. He was well off enough to purchase a new ones.

She snapped off several rosemary and lavender branches and covered her precious goods. She found more twine and tied everything into place. It was time to leave. There was not a minute to be wasted on second thoughts. She had no money for rent and the landlord would find a way of an alternative payment, of that she was certain.

The small trolley squeaked along the lane and Elle hoped it would not draw too much attention. The milk cart clattered along the more major road and she was grateful as it drowned out the squeaks and rattles that accompanied her. The long lane towards the town road was uphill at times and Elle huffed her way to the top. She became adept at holding back the trolley on the downhill run. Despite being wet through, she was warm with the effort.

Grateful for the walks she had taken with her Grandmother, she knew of a shortcut to the beach. Earlham's shoreline was a place she knew well, and it was not a fashionable, busy side of town. Old farming ground turned to marsh had driven most folk away. It was the ideal area for Elle to set up a small camp and gather her thoughts. Far enough from her parent's debts.

An hour or so later found her walking along the wet coarse grass, gorse covered beach pathway .The trolley dipped and turned across each sandy hillock, and the backs of Elle's calves ached. The grasses scratched and caught at her skin but she was determined to find a safe haven. The area became more bleak, and unforgiving but she trudged onward. Her mind churned over emotional thoughts, wondering why her parents had been so heartless.

Thought upon thought exploded out explanations to justify their actions but in truth she knew they were simply selfish. They had never shown her love, in this situation they would have never helped her. Their answers would be for her to accept her lot. Elle shut out the thoughts as best she could but they battered away until the one person who would have helped, needed to hear her plea.

Please. Please. I need help. Grandmamma, can you hear me? I am so alone. What am I to do?

Aware that if she sat down and gave into the tears that threatened, she would never get up again, so Elle dragged her tired legs along the path worn away by sheep years previous. Each time she licked her lips she could taste the salty tang of the seaside as the wind rushed in with an enthusiasm that Elle lacked.

She did not have a clue where to head for but decided to put her trust in fate. Belief in her Grandmother's guiding hand became so intense she drew strength from the thought and shushed all others to silence. Her goal was to find a clump of trees to give her shelter from the North Sea winds.

At last, miles away from the main entrance to the beach, she came across a rundown shepherd shelter. Rundown was the polite term for the building but Elle's gratitude in finding it exceeded any insults she would normally have used. The floods were too many over the years, and the farmers gave up working the land, now the shelter was no longer used. Time had hardened the land after the farmers tried to dig ditches and drain the area, but nothing of value grew there anymore. So, they simply abandoned it, and their makeshift buildings. This building had most certainly been abandoned.

Elle looked at the hut, a desolate sight. The door was off its hinges, and the window shutter had been rusted into place. Birds nested in every crevice in view and unidentifiable droppings laid around the entrance.

Undeterred, Elle stepped inside the large room and the rank smell hit her, with no other choice the building would suit her needs for the night. Large stones had dropped from the walls, and damp was evident upon the floor. Rain trickled down one wall, and puddled in the corner.

She dragged the trolley inside to prevent it from a further soaking, and walked behind a sandy mound around the back of the small building. No evidence of any sheep could be seen. The only living creatures she could see were the gulls as they swooped into the sea, their aim to catch a fish or two. Their cat-like screams grew louder upon a successful feast.

Reassured there were no threats to her safety in the surrounding area, Elle gathered a few branches and placed them in the small inglenook fireplace inside the shelter. With only a few strikes left in the tinderbox and two tapers, Elle crossed her fingers the fire would spark into life first time. She had been lucky yesterday and hoped her luck would hold today. It did.

Billowing smoke blew back into the room with full gusto. Choking, silently Elle cursed the bird who nested inside the chimney. She assessed the situation outside and found a small sloped roof around the back. It meant she could climb onto the rugged stones that stood out from the wall and gradually reach the roof area surrounding the chimney. The task proved difficult as she lost her footing a few times where the rain made moss and algae extra slippery but with dogged determination, she reached the top. With a long handle from her trolley hoard, she poked the nest further down the chimney. A plume of smoke and then flames told her the nest had caught fire, and proved the inner chimney was dry.

After a few seconds a steady trickle of smoke eased its way out of the chimney top. The lack of door allowed most of the smoke to dissipate from inside, and order was restored to Elle's eventful morning.

In need of a warm drink she placed her pot outside to capture rainwater pouring away in rivulets from roof. Boiled rainwater would do as a temporary measure until she gained her bearings, it would be different than the spring water she had been used to pumping from the village but with lavender and rosemary infused it would satisfy her need.

Soaked to the skin, she decided to gather what she could before she settled down and dried her clothing. She left the water to boil and headed for the shore. The full tide rushed back and forth to the sand in a furious hurry, and taking care not to fall into the full tide Elle reached out with her jar in the hope of snatching a crab or two. If she fell into the sea along this part of the coast, she knew from her Grandmother's warnings that the current would whisk her away. There would be no chance of survival, and despite her situation, Elle did want to live.

A small rock pool caught her eye where the water was not so deep, and she scrambled over the slimy rocks to take a peek at the contents, her crabbing efforts failed, and she needed to get back to the hut. A dried out starfish sat upturned on the top of one rock. Not sure if it would be edible, Elle decided it could stay where it was. However the small brown shrimps that swam happily around the pool would make a tasty morsel, and Elle grabbed her jar and scooped out several, enough for a mouthful or two. Any amount would keep her sustained until she could find work. A clump of curly kale and marsh samphire were also tugged from their resting place.

Back at the hut she made her drink, and placed her findings into the pot on the fire, a casserole of sorts bubbled away, and with her clothes steaming over the handle of her trolley, Elle sipped her warm drink.

After she had eaten the rain eased off to a weak drizzle, and she decided to take a walk around the area for more foodstuffs, driftwood and anything else that might come in useful. The shelter was to be home for a short time and she had to adapt to her environment. For one split second she thought of her parents, then brushed the thought aside. They had given no consideration to her or her welfare. Elle was on her own in the world, and had to face her fears and sorrow with strength. The strength she fancied she inherited from her beloved Grandmother.

CHAPTER 5

New Beginnings

The door Elle propped up with thick branches overnight, fell with a crash. Dust and debris sprayed her as she jumped from her makeshift bed.

'Who's there?' She called out in the serious hope there was nobody at all outside.

Please don't let it be the landlord. Calm down. How could he find you here?

'Stanley Orris.' Came the surprise response from a deep masculine voice.

'Stay where you are. Do not come in.' Elle called as she pulled on her chemise and dress. She rushed to the door and peeked outside. She couldn't see anyone.

'Err, Stanley. Stanley Orris?' She called out.

'Over here.' Came the reply from the right hand side of the hut.

'What do you want?' Elle called back.

'Why are you here?' The voice called back its own question.

Impatient with the whole affair, Elle stepped out. 'Come around where I can see you.'

Elle heard a strange shuffling sound, and eventually Stanley Orris came from his hiding place.

'You gave me a scare. I sheltered here for the night. I...'

Elle stopped talking as a young male limped towards her. He carried a bucket in one hand and the other was tucked inside his black jacket pocket. His dark, patched clothing indicated working class labourer. He leaned heavy to the right and a large, red jagged scar ran from his right eyebrow down to his chin, just clipping the edge of his lips.

'Why are you here? Are you lost?' He asked.

'Not exactly. What have you got in the bucket? Elle changed the subject. She did not want to give too much away. The less people knew, the less they could talk about her. It was safer that way.

'Crabs.' Was the response to her question. 'Do you eat crabs?'

The wind whistled around the hut and Elle began to shiver. A crab would be a treat fit for a queen, but she knew if she was to stand any chance of obtaining one she would have to be friendly to her visitor.

'It's freezing out there. You can come inside if you like. I have a small fire burning.'

She returned inside and waited for the shuffle of feet to start again. There was nothing attractive about the male entering the room, and Elle sensed she was in no danger, he bought with him an air of calm.

'Please. Sit. There, on the mattress, I have nothing else suitable I am afraid. My name is Elle. Elle Buchanan.' She went to hold out her hand but made a pretence of rubbing her hands warm. He did not appear to be able to hold the bucket, and shake her hand, she had no desire to embarrass the man.

'So what are you doing here, Elle Buchanan?'

Elle walked over to the bucket as he placed it onto the floor.

'Gosh. There are a lot in here. Did you catch them all this morning?'

Stanley shook his head. 'I earned them.'

'How did you earn them? What is your work? I took you for a farm hand, not a fisherman.' Elle could not imagine him capable of any work with his crippled legs. 'Forgive me, that sounded rude, what I meant was ...'

'I clean the fishing smacks in exchange for a bucket of the catch. Today they had more crabs than fish. Mother will be pleased. Fond of crabs she is.' Sidney interrupted.

Elle, pleased with how she had managed to move the conversation away from her again, perched herself onto one of the larger pieces of driftwood by the hearth and relaxed against the wall.

'Where do you live? Close by?'

'Not far. A cottage on the farm. Mother works in the house. General help. My father died there in an accident. It was the son's fault so the family feel obliged to keep a roof over our heads.'

'Was that how you became injured? Were you in the accident? I mean...'

Stanley pulled his arm out of the pocket. Elle recoiled when she saw the shrivelled skin at the end of a stump. 'I lost this when his cart ran over me. Drunk and out of control. My father tried to slow his horse down, but the boy whipped him and he fell. The horse trampled him to death. I was nearly there, but the family had me tended to, and the son was sent away.'

Elle regained her composure. 'I am sorry about your hand. Does it hurt?'

She rose to place another piece of wood on the fire.

Stanley put his arm back into the pocket. 'No. No feeling at all. Frustration gets me sometimes, but no pain. Enough about me. How come a young girl is hiding out in this place? Where's your folks?' Stanley looked around the room and back at Elle waiting for a reply.

Elle knew she could not delay the questions any longer. It pained her to speak the truth, but she had to face facts. Besides, she needed help.

'My parents have abandoned me. They left home owing the landlord a lot of rent. I tried to find them but they took all their belongings and left without a word. The landlord is a nasty piece and I had to flee for my safety.' She felt her bottom lip tremble and turned to the bucket again.

'I am sorry to hear that. So you are homeless? Do you have family to help?'

'Do you think I would have spent the night in this place if I had?' Elle snapped back with a wide sweep of her hand.

Stanley shook his head. 'My apologies. Do you really have nowhere to go?'

Elle looked to the floor, the dreaded tears threatened to weaken her resolve not to feel sorry for herself. 'No. This is it. The only place I could find. I knew the area and hoped I would go unnoticed. Please do not tell anyone about me. I feel safe here, I also think I am safe with you and am certain I can trust you to help me. Should I need it, of course.'

'I cannot give you a roof over your head on the farm, but I know a place better than this. What I mean is that the door is on its hinges and it belongs to nobody so far as I can tell. It will suit you until you are on your feet again. It is further along the path but not too far. I can take you there if you wish. I used to sit in there when I was coming to terms with this. You can trust me. Believe me, I know what it is to need a safe haven.' Stanley touched his face.

Elle's heart went out to her new friend. He had known her for no more than an hour and was prepared to help.

'Yes. Yes please, I would appreciate your help. Another night in this shelter is not something I relish, but needs must.'

Stanley picked his bucket of crabs and moved them to one side. I can pick these up on the way home. We will pop one in your pot for your supper. Come along then, help me roll this mattress.'

The small cottage sat nestled amongst three bare trees and had a broken-down fence marking its boundary. It looked shabby but habitable from the outside. Elle's heart fluttered with anticipation. It certainly looked much better than the shelter she had just left. Her fingers itched to draw the area, the cottage had character.

Stanley opened the door and turned to her wrinkling his nose.

'Dead cat I think is the aroma of the day. It will need a scrub out.'

'Don't worry about smells. I can freshen up a room. Let me in so I can see.' Elle pushed past him impatiently. Stanley burst out laughing.

'In a hurry are we?'

A small sink area, a fireplace and a small cubbyhole designed for storage, greeted her. Another small room to one side appeared to have been designed as the sleeping quarters, there was a sturdy truckle bed in one corner. The windows were intact and when Elle closed the door the winds were shut out. Only a small whistle showed there to be a small gap underneath.

'Oh, Stanley. It will be perfect. Are you sure there is no-one who will want a rent payment from me? I cannot pay anything at the present time, but I do hope to find work.'

'As I said, I don't think it belongs to anyone local. No-one has been here for years. I put the chair and table in here for the times when I came to sit. If you wish to stay, it is time to test out the fire.'

'I will stay, most definitely, and after the trouble I had yesterday, I am rather pleased you are here to assist.' Elle relayed the tale of the bird nest. Stanley roared with laughter while she described how she climbed the walls to the roof, and Elle could not help to like him a little more.

After Stanley left with a promise to return the next day to check on her welfare, and ensure she made it through the night with no unwanted intruders or escapades of any kind, Elle took stock of her situation. If left alone to live in the building she might have solved her housing problem. Crossing her fingers, she sent a prayer asking for there to be no owner of the building wanting funds in return for her living there.

She made a list in her mind of things to do and consider. The next item on the agenda would be work for her food. She made a mental note to ask Stanley whether he knew of any big houses in the area. Somewhere she might get a position.

The half candle flickered on the table and Elle ate the crab she cracked with a stone earlier in the evening. She spent her afternoon boiling seawater with lavender to clean around the place she consider her home. Using clumps of dried out grasses as cloths, she wiped away the undesirable aroma. Contented, Elle climbed onto her mattress airing in front of the fire. She was too cold to use the other room. In there she stored her pull-along with its precious contents. Stanley laughed when she pulled it into the cottage but Elle said until she felt more secure she was not prepared to lose them. He stopped smiling when she reminded him they were her only worldly goods.

CHAPTER 6
A Friend Indeed

Morning brought with it wind and rain. Fierce weather which refused to subside, and lightning flashed streaks of yellow and red across a multi-grey sky. Elle shivered as she pulled on her clothing. The fire was still alight and she was thankful for the stack of drift wood she accumulated the day before, and she added several pieces and enjoyed the warmth around her legs. The door rattled at times, and startled her but it stayed shut, and the kitchen window proved to be watertight. Elle went into the back room, and pulled out a few personal items, including her small collection of drawings and laid them on the table. Her grandmother's brooch sat beside them.

'I am sure you will forgive me, Gran, but I will have to pawn this.' She ran her finger over it lovingly. 'I am desperate thanks to your child. How could you both be so different? Oh how I miss you.' She spoke out loud as if her Grandmother was in the room. It made the wretched feeling of loneliness a little less severe.

A hefty bang on the door followed by a shout from Stanley saved her from more self-pity. She rushed to the door and was greeted by his crooked smile.

'So you made it through the night then.' He grinned back at her.

'I certainly did, thanks to you. This rain is a nuisance though, and the storm jangles my nerves. I had hoped to look around the outside. Mind, it will top up the barrel. Far better than sea water.'

'Did you enjoy your crab?'

'I did. It was most generous of you.'

'Not at all. You were in need and I had plenty. I sold all bar two. Mother and I enjoyed them. I am grateful to the boys on the quay. They allow me to hold my head up and help mother. Not one of them treats me like a cripple. They say I am a time-saving help. Talking of helping. Here, help me unload this.'

Stanley indicated to a cloth sack by his feet.

'Careful of the eggs in there. I managed to get them this far intact don't you be breaking them now!'

Elle rushed to the sack.

'Eggs? Oh, Stanley you truly are a friend. I will pay you when I can.'

'No need. They are laid by hens all over the place, and sit free for the taking around the farm. Half a dozen won't be missed.'

He unloaded the eggs onto the small bench beside the sink. Elle watched him produce various items and pinched herself to remind her it wasn't a dream. A small pat of butter and a cob of bread were placed on two new plates. A chipped china cup, tin mug, knife, fork and spoon, were next. They had been wrapped in a small muslin square. A rolled up blanket was unravelled and waved around like a flag and to Elle's delight a brown patched skirt and cardigan were the last of his gifts.

'They might be a little on the large side, but they are not being used. Shame they should go to waste.'

'They are marvellous, but won't your mother miss them?' Elle snuggled her face into the soft woollen garment.

Stanley shook his head. 'Not hers. These have laid about the outer barns since the seasonal workers left. No-one has claimed them so now they are yours. Warmer than the flimsy gown you are wearing today. I will keep my eyes open for better footwear. The slippers you have on now are not going to see you through winter.'

'Stanley. How can I ever thank you? Why are you helping me? I cannot and, um well...will not give you anything.' Elle looked to the floor, and hoped he would understand the meaning she tried to get across. He had to realise she was not ready to repay him in kind.

Stanley laid the sack on the back of her chair. He straightened his body as best he could.

'Do I look like a man who wants something from you? Fear not Miss Buchanan. I want no repayment —of any kind. When I had my accident folk looked after me in a way I never knew existed. I am simply doing the same for a fellow man-or woman-in need.'

Elle moved across the room and touched his arm. 'I am sorry if I offended you. It's just been such a hectic few days of worry, and here you turn up helping me. Bill, a man in Colchester helped me because his daughter had run away. He hoped someone would help her. I have had kindness bestowed on me by strangers yet my own parents abandoned me. Forgive me.'

Stanley gave her his lopsided grin and slipped off his coat. He moved to the table and picked up her drawings one by one.

'These your pa's?'

'No. Mine.'

'I mean did he draw them?'

'No. I did.' Elle said shyly.

'I am envious. That is a talent to be proud of indeed. They would fetch a bob or two in town. Not sure about this one though. Mayhap it might. Who is it, your pa?' He held up the etching of the man she had drawn on the bed at the hotel. Grateful he was draped with sheets, Elle took it from Stanley and placed it back into the box.

'Not my father. Someone who showed me kindness the same as you. Despite his attire, it is not what you might imagine.' She hoped her cheeks weren't as pink as they felt. The picture embarrassed her but equally she was proud of each line and stroke. It was one of her best drawings.

'Another Stanley, eh? Well he comes out a sight fairer of face than I do and that's a fact.'

Elle looked up sharply. 'You should not think like that. Your face tells a story.'

Stanley laughed. 'A story of a cartwheel, a large horse's hoof and a one-handed man.'

'Don't be so glib. I will draw you one day and you will see what I see. Now how about a bit of toast. This weather is not easing up.'

'Thank you, but I have already eaten and must be on my way. T'is a fair walk to Harwich. Mind, the wind will blow me along today. I will give you a look when I have finished. Um, just a thought. I wonder. Would you consider selling one of your pictures? There is an artist in Church Street who might be interested. And without wishing to offend, you could do with a coin in your pocket. This one, the one of the boats on the water, now that is an interesting picture.'

Elle looked at her small pile of treasures. The one Stanley held in her hand was one of her first, but not one of her favourites. 'If you think you could interest someone into purchasing it, then please do try. Should you sell it, please keep something for your troubles.'

'There will be no need for that. I will get you the best price I can. Enough for a loaf of bread and a few potatoes, and more I shouldn't wonder.'

'Thank you, Stanley. Thank you from the bottom of my heart.'

'Away with you. Surely you would do the same if the roles were reversed?'

'I would try, Stanley. I would try.'

Elle watched Stanley walk away. It pained her to see him struggle along the dunes. She felt a warm glow of comfort knowing he was her friend. Then it dawned on her, he was her first friend. Even as a tiny girl she had never mixed with the village children. She had been forever dragged from pillar to post while her parents worked. Stanley was a special person in her new life.

Closing the door as he disappeared into the distance, Elle looked at the gifts he had brought her. Her stomach rumbled, reminding her to eat. She cut through the bread and spread a scraping of butter into each corner. Biting into the creamy slice, Elle closed her eyes in ecstasy.

Whoever sent Stanley to save me; thank you. Thank you.

After she had finished eating, she tried on her new clothes. They were large, but Elle twisted and tucked them to fit. Never had she owned such an outfit. Her hands traced over the pleats and brown rust coloured, patterned embroidery that had been stitched into hole-covering patches on the skirt. The deep brown cardigan was long, too long but she welcomed the warmth around her thighs. With her thin chemise, threadbare blouse and skirt underneath, winter seemed a little friendlier. If Stanley sold her picture for food, maybe he might be able to sell another and she could purchase a pair of sturdier boots. The prospect excited Elle. Her hand-me-downs from her mother were not serviceable, and with no stockings her feet ached with cold. She tried to see her reflection in the small glass window but to no avail. Regardless of what others might think she looked like, Elle felt every inch a lady in her new attire.

The wind died down and although it was grey outside, there was no sign of rain. Elle collected her cooking pot and took herself off for a walk around the area. The pot was heavy and Elle's arm ached. A lighter pot was one of the first things Elle intended to purchase.

The sea tossed and rolled back exposing its sandy base. The tide was going out and Elle knew there would be fresh whelks and winkles lying around. Many days with her Grandmother had been spent winkle picking and placing them in jars. They steeped in vinegar for days and made her mouth tingle when she took her first bite. Although she had no vinegar, Elle felt sure she would enjoy them just the same. A fresh green batch of seaweed straddled a rock, and she placed it in the pot. The grey-green leaves of the sea kale made a pretty picture and grew freely along the drier parts of the dunes. Elle picked only enough for one day, happy in the thought there would be plenty more where that came from. Satisfied she had collected enough food for supper, she made her way back to the place she dared to consider home.

***

Stanley battled against the wind. Elle's drawing puzzled him, the man was someone he recognised but she showed signs of fear. Despite wanting to know more about the connection between the couple, Stanley opted to respect her privacy, and keep what was obviously some form of secret. The girl had whisked the drawing away, and hidden it amongst others within seconds. Hers was not a situation Stanley wanted to be in, and if the man in the sketch was part of her downfall, then she needed a friend to prevent any further upset in her life. From the moment the thought appeared, Stanley vowed to be that friend.

CHAPTER 7
One Step Forward

Elle heard Stanley's whistle before she saw him. He said he had taken to giving her the signal so she would not be frightened by his sudden appearance. Although Elle teased it was so she could heat water for herb tea.

Stanley said since he had been drinking her concoctions he felt more energetic, and his joints ached far less. Whether it was true or not, Elle was pleased he enjoyed her company enough to stop and join her for a cup.

He tapped on the door and let himself in. When Elle was drawing she didn't like to be disturbed, so she had given Stanley permission to enter unless told otherwise. The scenes she worked were easy enough to create from inside the small house on blustery days. One window overlooked the craggy rocks, and outlying land away from the sea, so all options of landscapes were well and truly covered.

When Stanley sold two of her pictures, her treasured purchases were a small drawing pad and two sticks of real charcoal and a lead pencil. The owner of the art shop was keen to see more of her work. Elle spent time drawing seashore scenes in readiness of their first meeting. She also purchased a pair of second-hand boots that had hardly been worn, a small sack of potatoes and two new pots but her artist materials were her extravagance, essential to her future.

'My, you are cheerful this afternoon.' Elle acknowledge Stanley without looking up from her table.

'I have news. 'Stanley replied.

Elle finished the piece she was working on and turned around. 'News? What sort of news?'

Moving towards her, Stanley looked to the water pot bubbling on the fire.

'Mm, I have worked harder than I thought. A break is just what I need.' She stretched her arms, and moved to the kitchen area. 'So what news do you bring, mysterious friend?' Elle held out two mugs containing a variety of herbs while Stanley poured in the water.

'Angus, the artist. Angus Argyle. He wants to meet you.' Stanley sipped his tea and winced as it burned his lips. He set aside the mug and picked up her drawing. 'He said anyone with a talent such as yours shouldn't be hidden away. And before you say anything, I have kept my promise. All he knows is that you are young and shy.'

'Shy is not one of my qualities, but thank you for keeping your word. So when am I to meet this, Angus Argyle? What a strange name. He is not from the county of Essex with a name such as that, I'll vouch. It sounds foreign.' Elle cleared away her few artist materials into a box Stanley had found for the purpose.

'He is from Scotland. The North. A quiet man. I have not an artistic bone in my body, but even I can see he has created some magnificent pieces. You will get great pleasure from them. We could visit tomorrow if you wish. Meet me at the end of the pathway. I do not have to wash down the smacks until the afternoon. Watch for Old Mosses' red smack going out on the full tide. When you see it near the Felixstowe mouth, I will be waiting.'

'I can't thank you enough, Stanley. How exciting. And for a change, I have a small token to give to you.'

Elle handed him a small round loaf. Stanley looked at it and smiled. 'You have made good use of the flour I see. You should really keep this for yourself, you have so little, Elle. I do appreciate the thought.'

'It is a seaweed loaf. My grandmother taught me how to bake it, and I can spare a small loaf for a friend. Please take it, share it with your mother.'

Stanley slipped the loaf inside his coat. 'Thank you, Elle. We will enjoy it with our supper. It is a generous gift and smells delicious. I did ask around the staff at the farm if they knew of any houses hiring at the present time. Sadly there is not, so far as they are aware. I will keep searching for you.'

'If I can earn from my drawings enough to feed me, and no demands for rent are made, I could live a comfortable life here. I am in a better situation than I was three weeks ago, thanks to you.'

'You are a survivor and a fighter that is certain, Elle Buchanan. Now I will bid you goodbye, as my mother will fret should I be late. Until tomorrow.' Stanley replaced his cap and shuffled off down the pathway. Elle no longer stood watching him leave, it always saddened her, so she closed the door against the elements and her friend. As she leaned against the door and gazed at the rich amber flames in the hearth, Elle reflected on recent events. She was content in the small home, and now she was ready to face the outside world.

An artist. I am to meet a real artist.

With renewed enthusiasm, she pulled out her drawings. Sea grasses with rocky backdrops were all very well, but Elle hungered for more. Each day she saw new shapes, vivid colours she had never noticed before.

The sea with its dramatic surroundings absorbed her, and fascinated her critical eye. Black charcoaled scribbles that sold for a few coins kept her in food, they saved her life, yet she yearned to find out how to use different materials and take the risk of only selling the occasional painting. Tomorrow she would ask Angus Argyle more about her passion.

CHAPTER 8
An Artist's Eye

Wind whipped around the corner of the seafront, and Elle struggled to stay on her feet. Stanley huddled beside a large boulder when she greeted him with a puffed hello. Bracing herself against the rock to regain her breath, she marvelled at the waves crashing against the edge of the shore.

'Gosh, it is a strong gale today. Old Mosses' boat tossed about as it set off around the bend.'

Stanley nodded and said something, but Elle could not hear against the howling wind. Stanley tugged at her sleeve and took the drawings she clutched for fear of them blowing away. He tucked them into an inside pocket. Still unable to speak to each other, he pointed in front of them. She took hold of his arm and the pair-heads down-battled their way along the pathway towards Dovercourt, and then onto Harwich.

Turning a corner the winds dropped slightly and the roaring sounds in Elle's ears settled to a hushed whooshing sound.

'I love the sea, but it can be a vicious beast at times.' Stanley said as he straightened his cap.

'It is fortunate I have no bonnet to wear for I fear it would look a little worse for wear after that walk.' Elle let go of his arm and rearranged the small blanket around her shoulders.

'Have you lived here all your life or are you an outsider?' She asked Stanley. Their conversations usually ended up around her problems, and she rarely had chance to learn more about her supportive companion.

'Born and bred. Mother was born on the farm, and my father was a seasonal labourer from Manningtree. He and mother fell in love one summer and he gained a permanent position. I came along three years later.'

'So why don't you work on the farm? This is a long walk each day, and washing down fish guts can't be pleasant.'

'It started out as an exercise for my leg. Every day I walked the extra mile, until I found myself in Harwich. My chats with the men working the quay became part of my survival process. They treated me like a man, not a cripple. On the farm they pity me. I do a few odd jobs, but to be honest the work is too much for me. Mother works hard enough, so our place is secure. And as you can appreciate, the fish are an acceptable form of payment.'

The pair walked and chatted about their childhood happenings, and Elle was surprised when they crossed over into the entrance of Harwich and its narrow streets. They passed the large lighthouse and Elle tucked an image into the back of her mind to be released on paper later that day.

'Here we are then.' Stanley brought her out of her daydream.

A small windowed building sat on the corner of George Street. It sported grimy windows and a paint- chipped front door. However, Elle saw a quaintness about the place.

Stanley moved around the corner and beckoned her with a grin. Elle rushed to his side, and the sight before her made her heart leap. A clean, large paned window glistened before them. Through the window she could see a range of paintings and drawings that would delight any eye. And there in the centre of a group of small drawings were two of her own. Tears welled up and Elle put her hands to her mouth to prevent the squeals of delight that threatened to burst forth.

'Stanley. Look. My work. On display.' The words tumbled out as Elle tried to compose herself.

Stanley lifted the latch and stood back to allow her through the doorway.

'So they should be, you are an artist.' He said above the tinkling of the shop bell.

Elle turned and gave him a shy smile, before she walked slowly around the large room. New smells filled her nostrils, and she inhaled deeply.

'So this is what an artist's studio smells like. Oh, just take a look at those pictures. Stanley this is magical.'

Colours of every kind imaginable shone back at her from large canvasses. She longed to reach out and touch them. Every subject possible had been painted. Even the small half naked female staring back at her was acceptable in Elle's eyes. She was a true piece of art.

'I bet her mother has never seen this one.' Elle giggled at her boldness.

Stanley grinned. 'Behave yourself, Miss Buchanan.'

'Miss Buchanan? So your little artist has shed her shyness and graced me with her presence-eh?'

Elle moved to Stanley's side as a thin male old enough to be her father entered the room. His hair was sticking out at all angles and the colour of straw with red tinges. His accent was the strangest she had ever heard.

'Angus. Allow me to present Miss Elle Buchanan. Elle meet the artist, Angus Argyle.'

The man held out his hand, took Elle's and put it to his lips. She felt a rush of blood flow to her cheeks. The man was either deranged or insane. He was treating her as if she was titled, not a scrap of a girl dressed in rags. The man fascinated her. He wore, what could only be described as a shepherds' smock covered in paint smudges.

'Pleased to meet you sir.' For the first time in her life Elle was lost for words but manners were required for the man who saw worth in her scribbles.

'Did you see your pictures on display?' Angus gestured towards the small plinth where her work sat in all its glory. 'I sold them today. They are going to the home of a fine lady. So my dear girl, you had better produce a few more. Popular little drawings I think they will become. Ideal souvenir gifts. Worth the few coins I gave you, most definitely.'

Elle found her courage and stepped towards the drawings. 'I can bring you some more sir. Stanley has two on his person, should you wish to purchase them. I wanted to ask your opinion on my choice of shading and angles.'

Angus Argyle rushed to Stanley. He held out his hand. 'Show me boy. Show me.'

Stanley handed him the pictures and Elle stood watching while the artist frowned and chewed upon his top whiskers.

'How do you manage to create such simple beauty with charcoal? Such bland colours and yet still you bring to life the ocean and her surroundings. Talent. Raw talent.'

'Thank you, sir, but you flatter and tease me.' Elle walked to a painting of a tree laden with delicate pink-white blossom. 'This sir, is a work of an artist. Such pretty flowers.'

'Pah. Pretty flowers. An apple tree in blossom painted to attract the frilly, fussy women of the parish. I can paint them in my sleep. You could too, but that would be a wicked waste of your eye. Paint from your soul, not what you think should be hanging on walls. Paint what you feel inside. That is true art. You do not know the true value of your talent yet, but I tell you, one day your name will be known. But it is up to me to help you realise your talent.'

'I cannot paint sir. My only materials are the charcoal pieces and papers you kindly sent with Stanley. That is the only way I know how to get down what I see. Sometimes I want to capture colour and splash it across my work. It frustrates me when I see the gold shades of sunset and have to let them die in black smudges on paper. My talent is as limited as my tools.'

Elle looked wistfully at the paintings that surrounded her. Angus pulled out a chair and indicated to Stanley to sit. He left the room and returned with two more.

'Mrs Wright is coming through with a light lunch. We could sit in my boring rooms but I feel you would prefer this room, young lady. You describe your angst as prettily as you etch your visions. Do you want to learn a little more about the materials I use?' Angus laughed as Elle nodded with great enthusiasm. 'Very well we will eat first and when Stanley leaves for work, we can get down to business.'

After a meal of eggs with pressed tongue, washed down with a sweetened milk, Elle had her first lesson of using a brush to paint with and how to sketch out her work using a lead pencil. Angus praised her every step of the way. By the end of the session, Elle was saddened to have to return to using charcoals again, but knew they were her bread and butter materials.

'You grasped the basics well, my dear. Very well. Bring me four new drawings in a few days. Next week is Christmastide and your work would make perfect gifts. Now forgive me. I have to finish commissioned pieces before then. If you walk to the end of this street you will find Stanley on one of the fishing boats to the right hand side of the quay. It was a pleasure to meet you and I look forward to working with you in the future.'

'Sir, the pleasure has been all mine. Your kindness is overwhelming. Thank you.' Elle and Angus shook hands.

'The pleasure has been all mine. I have not been kind. Your drawings sell. I earn from them. A selfish pleasure, believe me. So until – let us say- Thursday?'

'Yes. Thursday. I look forward to sharing more work with you.'

Elle left the shop and faced the blustery winds with a renewed energy. Life had turned for the better. Her mind was swimming with the information she gleaned from Angus. He was a patient man and explained things so simply she never struggled once. She could have listened to him for hours. He explained words outside of her simple vocabulary, and at no time did Elle feel inferior.

The quayside was busy with men passing buckets, pulling ropes and generally going about their business. The smell of fish filled the air and the gulls screeched their eager call. The noise reminded Elle that there was life outside of her small world. Weathered faces grinned gummy smiles, youthful ones winked and Elle knew she had to come back and capture each character on canvas one day. When she caught up with Stanley, she chatted on about how she would save for paints and canvas with the money from Angus. It was not until they arrived back at the pathway close to home did she realise Stanley had hardly said a word.

'My tongue has rambled for miles. My apologies dear friend. Your ears must be bored of my endless chatter.'

'Not at all. It is wonderful to hear you excited and I am pleased you and Angus can support each other.'

Elle threw open her arms in a moment of impulsive expression, and excitement. Her voice high-pitched with enthusiasm.

'I am blessed with new friends. How different my life is becoming. Once I was full of fear, now my heart swells with joy. I must get home and start on some new work. Thank you again.' She hugged Stanley in an unladylike embrace, and he laughed aloud.

'Elle, you must not be so free with your embraces around me. If we are seen people will talk. I want you to have a reputation as a famous artist, not as a lady of ill-repute. Please allow me space to breathe, and let me on my way.'

Elle giggled, and stepped away from her friend. They parted company with a polite hand-shake and a mock curtsy from Elle. Stanley pulled his collar around his neck, and headed home. Elle put her head down to battle against the swirling winds, and scurried along the pathway taking care of the large puddled holes, eager to get back to drawing. So many ideas raced around her head. Inspiration knocked loudly, and Elle hoped she could create new images from her ideas.

***

Stanley stopped and turned. He watched the swirling hair of his friend, dance in the wind. Hair he longed to run his fingers through. He watched her hips sashay below a tiny waist. A waist he suppressed urges to embrace and draw into him. Stanley publicly declared his affection for Elle as nothing more than friendship, however, his heart kept his secret. He had fallen in love but would never share his feelings, with his disability and looks, he would never handle the rejection. His vow to be a good friend, a brother-like figure in her life, remained his goal.

CHAPTER 9

Festive Feelings

The grey days did not hold back Elle's visual frenzy. She worked on improving herself in everyday life, and her artistic life. She watched and mimicked the voices and mannerisms of young ladies taking the air along the promenade. She worked her charcoals to blunt stubs. Every corner she turned a new subject would capture her imagination, and hours were spent completing pictures for Angus' customers.

Always the supportive tutor, he guided her through long lessons in shading and outline. Elle absorbed and hung onto every word. Never would he have such a willing pupil. She was also a very determined young woman in her private life. She vowed to improve her vocabulary, appearance, and become independent from the restrictions and restraints of Victorian society.

Her strength improved with the foods she ate and the walks to and from Harwich. Her energy levels enabled her to stay awake for longer hours and work on her mini projects. Not one gull landed that wasn't etched on her pad. She invested in new charcoals and a drawing pad each time she received payment from her sales. Angus gave her a small discount despite her protestations that he was teaching her for free, and that was enough.

'Have you eaten?' Stanley approached her as she sat on a dune drawing a fishing smack bobbing on the water. 'Excuse me, Miss Buchanan. I asked if you have eaten.'

Elle turned to Stanley and he laughed. His face crinkled around his scar, and made Elle giggle. 'What are you laughing at? You have made me laugh and I don't know why.'

'Me thinks you have eaten your charcoal sticks for breakfast.' Stanley pointed to her face. 'You have black smudges around your lips and on your cheeks. What, in the name of Neptune, have you been doing?'

Elle rubbed around her face in an attempt to rid it of the said smudges. Stanley nodded and shook his head in appropriate places when she successfully removed each dirty mark.

'It is where I am blending with my finger, then dampening my finger for a darker effect. Angus taught me a new technique yesterday. How are you? And why are you asking if I have eaten?'

Stanley sat down beside her and watched her hands fly across the page as she created another new picture. 'Because, Elle, you tend to forget to eat if I am not around to remind you.' He held up his hands as if in defence of his words, when Elle turned to face him. Her mouth creased in objection.

'Of course I eat. Don't I look a picture of health to you? I certainly feel it. I have food in store, and plenty of it for your information, Mr. Orris.' Elle's face lost its serious look and she grinned back at him. 'Please do not fret, Stanley. I have eaten. Eggs and bread. Tonight I shall find a feast to satisfy me.'

'Tonight? I think not my dear friend. Today you are invited to my home. Mother cannot bear the thought that I have a friend alone on Christmas day. I have not told her much. Only that you are an orphan who I have been helping with the assistance of Angus Argyle. I felt it better to mention his name, seeing how you live alone. I did make enquiries about your home, and nobody seems to have a claim on the place. Mother says you should remain there if it is warm and safe. Please say you will join us. There will only be the two of us. So no-one else will ask questions. Mother has promised to keep your presence quiet. I told her about the old landlord, and how he made your life uncomfortable. She is a good woman and I trust her word. Please, again I ask you accept her invitation. We have rabbit and a plum pudding.'

Elle stood up. Her movement was so abrupt she startled Stanley and he too scrambled to his feet.

'Christmas day? How have I forgotten Christmas day? Oh, Stanley, I would love to meet your mother. Let me clean my face. Come, come and choose a picture. A gift for your mother. I heard the church bells ringing, but my mind was focused on my drawing. Mind, I have not attended church for several years. Grandmother would take me.' Elle words tumbled over each other in excitement. She linked her arm through Stanley's and they took a slow amble back to her home.

Elle washed her face and tidied her hair. She brushed down her clothing to free it from sand and grass seeds. While Stanley looked through a small selection of pictures, Elle tucked the surprise gift she had for Stanley under her blanket-cum-shawl.

A flash of sadness overcame her as they walked towards Stanley's home.

Christmas day. *Wherever you are my parents, I hope you give one small thought for your daughter.*

Elle's nerve seeped away with every step closer to the farm. Fields and buildings loomed closer and closer. Her heart pounded in her chest. She stopped walking and took a deep breath.

What is the matter with you? No evil landlord can find you here. Stanley is a good friend. His mother cannot be a bad woman to have invited you into her home. Why are you frightened?

'Do my ears deceive me? Have I become deaf?' Stanley shuffled around in front of her, just in time to see the tears that dripped unintentionally from her chin. 'Lord above, what has happened? Are you in pain? Elle pray tell me what is the problem?'

Elle looked at Stanley's face so full of concern. His eyes pained in fear she was in pain. It was too much to bear and the tears flowed freely. She made no attempt to stop them. Sobs overcame words she tried to force out. Reassuring words for her friend, that all was well.

He stood patiently with one arm on her forearm as if preventing her from running away. No forceful grip but just gentle reassurance that she was in safe hands. After a moment of silence, Elle composed herself.

'My apologies, Stanley. Your kindness and that of your mother moved me. My own parents...' her words trailed away as a fresh batch of tears threatened.

Stanley guided her to a wooden bench outside of the farm gates. He knelt in front of her on his good knee. Elle's sobs subsided as he spoke in gentle tones.

'Now listen to me. Your parents were selfish and uncaring. No amount of your protests and defensive arguments will persuade me otherwise, so do not try. Elle, I have a love for you. Not a romantic love. As a friend, and in no other manner. You are like a daughter-sister-friend, rolled into one. Our short friendship has been built on trust. Pure friendship. My mother has a love for me. An unconditional love. The love of a mother. Never once during my dark moods did she desert me. What I am endeavouring to say is this. No matter what you feel for your parents, do not let it eat into your heart and sadden you. They had a choice to cherish you forever, regardless of their situation. However, they chose to leave you defenceless and alone. Move forward with your life. Embrace a new future. Come now and meet Mother, she will bring a smile to your face and lighten your heart. I promise. Also my knee is complaining along with my back.' He struggled to his feet and stretched his legs.

Elle stood and kissed his cheek.

'Thank you. Your love and friendship is the best gift I could ever enjoy. You are right about my parents. They have hurt me deeply. It is time to store them as a childhood memory.' Elle took a deep breath. 'I am ready to meet your mother, if she has a heart half the size of yours, she is a wonderful person.'

The buildings surrounding the small cottage looked bright and cheery with their red brick and large windows of lace. Chickens clucked around their feet and a small dog ran amongst them.

'That's Tess. She is a gentle soul unless you are a rat. A feisty little terrier if ever we had one on the farm, that's for sure. Here we are. Ready?'

Elle nodded and looked up startled as the cottage door was flung wide open. Cooking smells like she had never smelt before, surrounded her. Saliva flowed into her mouth and she gulped with anticipation. A Christmas meal awaited. Since her grandmother's death she had not enjoyed a Christmas gathering. Her parents were not ones who celebrated special events.

'Why there you are. Come along both of you. Girl you look chilled to the bone, come. Sit.' A short plump woman with grey streaked hair stood in the doorway. Her cheeks cherry red and her eyes sparkling blue-green. A large white apron covered her ample bosom and a cloth cap perched upon her head, bobbing as she jostled them inside the warm room. 'Stanley. That's it my boy, help the girl with her bl–er-shawl.'

Elle felt a flush of embarrassment rise to her cheeks. She was so used to only being in the company of two men. Neither one would take note of the fact she was wore a blanket. Now, in the company of another woman, she felt shabby, a new sensation, and it made her feel uncomfortable. When she received her gift of clothing she vowed she wouldn't worry what people thought, but at this very moment she wished she had another gown.

I will save for one. A Sunday best.

'Oh do sit my dear.' Stanley's mother ushered her across the room. Elle smiled her thanks as she was placed into a large, comfortable seat by the fireside. Stanley had taken her blanket through to another room and Elle felt she should say something.

'Your home is very pleasant, Mrs. Orris. So cosy.' It was a good sized room and Elle could see it was well kept.

'Why thank you my dear. Here, drink this. It is a warm mead, not too strong but good to warm the cockles of your heart.' Stanley's mother place a steaming mug of honeyed-wine into Elle's hands.

Small blue and white plates lined one wall and Elle rose to get a closer look.

'Dutch. They are from Holland. Across the water. My husband had a friend who travelled over from a place called Rotterdam. Each time he came to England he brought me a gift. Sadly he died the year before the accident. My husband missed their friendship. I will confess to being a little sad about no more pretty blue plates. I cannot bring myself to eat off of them.'

Elle shook her head. 'No, never move them. They are perfect where they are. Such wonderful pictures on each one.'

Stanley re-entered the room. 'Admiring Mother's pride and joy? Talking of pride and joy. Ma, Elle has brought you a gift. Remember I told you she is an artist. This is one of her drawings.' Stanley glanced over at Elle. She felt slightly self-conscious and gave a weak smile.

'Oh you dear child. What a delightful gift. How talented you are. The fishermen from Harwich –a fine picture they make. I will find a place beside my plates. Thank you, my lovely. Thank you.'

Mrs. Orris embraced Elle with such a passion she thought she would stop breathing.

'You are welcome. Good tidings to you, and thank you for welcoming me into your home on such a special day.'

'A friend of Stanley's in need is more than welcome, and on any occasion. Now as it happens, I have a gift for you. And don't look so put out, son. I have not forgotten you. I will let you go first so there will be no sulking male at my table.' The woman giggled as she reached inside a large wooden box beside another chair.

'Sit down and close your eyes, Stanley.'

Laughing, Stanley did as he was told. His mother placed a brown paper package on his lap.

'Open them.'

Stanley obliged and Elle giggled as she watched him pull the twine bow undone. It amazed her how agile he was with one hand. Slowly he maneuvered his fingers around the paper to reveal something dark green. He lifted out the gift and gave a whoop of delight.

'A new waistcoat. How thick it is. Ma it is a beauty of a gift. Why thank you.'

He eased himself from the chair and kissed the beaming woman on the cheek. A twinge of envy ran through Elle in the form of a shiver, despite the warm room.

'My, it is handsome. Did you stitch it, Mrs. Orris? She enquired.

'I did. Every moment when Stanley was out of the door, I worked on it. The fabric came from a peddler who passed through during the summer. As soon as I saw it I knew what I would make. You deserve it for being such a good son.' Mrs. Orris returned the kiss.

Elle turned her head away from the scene before her. There was so much love between the two that she couldn't bear to watch. Envy moved into pain, the tears threatened again and she was determined not to let past memories spoil her day.

'Elle. I have a gift for you too. Close your eyes.'

'Me?'

'Yes, young lady, now do as I say. Eyes closed.'

Elle squeezed her eyes tightly. The rustle of paper tempted her to re-open them, but she was enjoying the moment of surprise.

'Keep them shut. No peeking.' Stanley teased.

The package was place on her lap.

'Ready? Now open.' Mrs. Orris instructed.

Elle opened her eyes to a brown paper package very much like Stanley's.

'I guess a green waistcoat.'

'Open it, Elle. No guessing will give you the answer.' Stanley encouraged.

Slowly she untied the twine, and spent a moment winding it around her fingers into a tidy knot. She held it out to Stanley. Mrs. Orris sat watching with a wide smile playing around her lips. Lifting the paper away from its contents, Elle gasped.

Colours stared back at her, every colour she could think of had been woven into a hooky bed-rug. A warm covering to brighten her home and keep her warm at night. A handcrafted piece of art.

'I am at a loss for words. What can I say? It is beautiful. Thank you so very much.' Elle made no attempt to stop the tears that flowed down her cheeks. They were happy tears.

'Now, now, no tears. You are most welcome, child. When Stanley described how you were living, I was driven to make you something useful. It does my heart good to see your face enjoy my work. Unfold it and find the other surprise.' Mrs. Orris said as she lifted the edges of the rug.

Peeking underneath Elle could see a flash of white. She unfolded the bed-rug and found a crisp white sheet and pillow slip. Both had been embroidered with her initials in a pastel blue thread. A delicate pink rose had been stitched beside them.

'Mrs. Orris. They are beautiful. What a thoughtful gift. Again I am lost for words. Thank you so very, very much.' Elle placed the items on the chair beside her and walked over to the woman who had given her so much. A stranger. Someone who had never met her before had sat stitching her initials into something to keep her warm and snug. She held out her hands in a gesture of friendship. She leaned forward and planted a kiss on the woman's cheek. At no moment did she feel self-conscious. It was the right thing to do. No words were needed.

'Can I give you my gift now?' Stanley interrupted the moment. He held out another brown paper package tied with twine. This time Elle pulled open the present slightly faster. Her eyes glistened and her jaw dropped with amazement. In her hands she held an artists' mixing tray, four paint brushes and a pallet knife. Inside the packet lay six tiny tubes of oil paints and two square canvas pieces.

'Oh, Stanley. The perfect gift. How did you..?'

'Angus helped me choose. He told me you had been shown a few techniques and without these they would be wasted.'

'But...'

Stanley held up his hand. 'No buts. They are an investment for your future. I am proud to be the person who has helped you on the road of success. So all I ask is you become famous and never forget me...us.' Elle noted his face flush and was touched by his speech.

'How could I ever forget you? I will do my best with regard to becoming famous.' Elle giggled. 'Thank you. Thank you both for such beautiful gifts. Again, I am lost for words.'

For a moment only the noise of the meat sizzling could be heard. Then Stanley gave a slight cough.

'I have never known Elle to be lost for words. It is a Christmas miracle indeed.' The friends laughed and Elle's joy rose. Then she remembered her gift for Stanley. When he had taken her blanket she had managed to hide it beside her seat.

Wrapped in a piece of sacking sat a gift she had spent many hours on. Her heart fluttered as she handed it to Stanley.

'This is my gift to you. I once told you I would draw you as I see you, not as you think people see you. Well, oh open it and you will see.'

Stanley laid the square packet on his lap. With the same deliberate movements as before, he lifted off the covering. He sat looking at the contents, then back at Elle. He glanced up at his mother and back at the gift.

'It is my first water colour. I sketched your face from memory and Angus guided me through each stage. Getting your skin colouring was a challenge. He also helped me make the frame from drift wood. Say something, Stanley. Please.'

Stanley looked up at her. His face had an expression she could not read. There were no tears but Elle wondered if he was going to cry. Bewildered she blurted out her frustration.

'You don't like it. Oh, no. It never occurred to me!'

'How can I not like it? Look at this mother. See how she sees me, how my dear friend sees this ragged face.' He handed the picture in its rustic frame to his mother.

'She has captured your eyes and smile well. This is truly a piece of art. Look at the shadows and colours. Elle you look at my son and see him as I do. Kind and gentle.'

Stanley held out his good hand to Elle.

'Thank you. Bless you.' He turned back to his mother. 'Is that goose cooked yet? I am famished.'

'Take this and put it in the back room. We will fix it to the wall tomorrow. Yes, the goose is waiting to treat us to a feast. A gift from the big house, and a fine one at that. Fetch the platter from the dresser, Elle. Yes, that one. Good girl.'

A feast was eaten by all three and Elle declared she would burst at the seams. Goose, parsnips, cabbage and potatoes had been devoured and a plum pudding had been savoured. Mead had been supped and before Elle knew it, it was time to make her way home.

'The light is fading. I should go home. Reluctantly I must leave you. I can never repay the kindness you have both shown me. Today is a day I will never forget. Thank you.'

Mrs. Orris wrapped a few items of food into a muslin cloth as she spoke. 'The pleasure was ours, Elle. You are a special friend of Stanley's and I like to think we can be friends. Please come and visit any time. And I should like to call on you one day. Take these for your meal tomorrow. And keep with your drawing, you truly have a talent worth sharing. Stanley will walk you back.'

'Thank you. Please come and visit any time you are free. If I am not at the cottage, I will be somewhere around drawing. Really, Stanley you do not have to see me home. It is warm and you are rested. I will see my own way.'

Stanley handed Elle her blanket.

'Please believe me when I say I need to walk you home. Mother's feast has filled my boots and I need to stretch my legs. Besides I have eggs for you and you will need me to carry your other package.'

Elle kissed Mrs. Orris on both cheeks and made no attempt to pull back as the woman embraced her. The moment was the perfect end to a perfect day. It was a mother's embrace, and one she had never experienced. Before tears could form, she pulled away and maneuvered Stanley out of the door.

'The air is crisp tonight. Your home is warm and pleasant, I feel guilty about you leaving to walk with me. Your mother is a wonderful woman, you are truly blessed.'

Their boots crunched along the crisp grass and clouds of cool breath floated ahead.

'It did her good entertaining you. My sister died when she was five years old. Mother never had another. She has a heart made for a daughter as well as this crippled son of hers. She will be a good friend, Elle. Allow her into your life and you will never regret it. Do not fear she will invade your privacy. Mother is a private person herself.'

Wind whistled along the pathway and salt spray dampened the pair as they hurried as best they could. Only the moon shone a light in-between cloud breaks. Both followed their instinct to guide them toward Elle's home.

'No glowing light to greet me, but at least the fire should still be alight.'

'I was thinking about the cottage. It is time you stamped your mark and made the place permanent. Or you find new accommodation.'

'I cannot imagine living anywhere else. Mayhap I should seek out the owner and offer rent. I would like a more secure home. My parents are no longer in the area. Of that I am convinced. I walked to Parkeston and the old home is alive with a new family. A stranger was tending the garden. I have to face facts.'

'As I mentioned before, there is no record of an owner. Talking of garden. If you are to stay, I will build you a raised vegetable bed. If we can manage to bring soil and manure from the farm, there is no reason why foodstuff shouldn't grow here. With the wood lying around the farm we could fence in an area. In spring I will fix a few slats around the bottom of the door and window to stop the draft.'

'That would be wonderful, Stanley. Thank you. I do believe I am meant to live here. It is perfect for me to paint in peace.' Elle laughed as the door creaked open. 'The extra wood around will come in handy. Howling winds are not a good companion on a dull day. Good. The logs have stayed alight. It is warmer in here than out there. I do not envy you walking back again.'

'Do not worry about me. A good walk helps strengthen my leg and aids my sleep at night. I will leave you to unpack your gifts. Thank you again for coming today. It meant a lot to mother and me.'

Elle shook her head. 'Thank you for having me. Without you and your mother, I would not have had Christmas day at all. It has been the best day of my year. Mind how you go home. Here take my oil lamp. Bring it back tomorrow. I have candles.'

'I will do that, thank you. Now goodnight and sleep well.'

Elle banked up the fire. She stored away her food treats in the appropriate places and then unwrapped her Christmas gifts.

She pulled away the worn sheets from her bed and laid out her new ones. She stuffed the old sheets inside the pillow slip, making it the first pillow she had ever slept upon. The coloured bed-rug brought new life to the corner of the room. Elle then unloaded her new artist materials on one side of the table. She traced a finger over them, longing to make a start on a new project.

'Tomorrow, I will seek out the ideal subject. Tomorrow I will work on becoming famous', Elle laughed out loud and spoke to no one but the shadows. 'First I must make use of my new bedding. It is going to be a warm, comfortable night for a change'.

CHAPTER 10
A New Year Dawns: 1866

Wind whistled around the cottage and Elle pulled the covers tight around her body. The snug new bed linen gave her warmth, and she could not have asked for a better gift. Rain lashed against the small window and Elle shifted around in her small bed. It was still dark outside and she was frustrated by the hour - and noises. Tortured by the tinny sounds of a metal pail receiving endless drops of rain, Elle grunted and called out to the heaving winds.

'Oh, let up, please. All I want to do is paint. How can I if you are battering the sunrise back to bed?'

A gentle glow from the fireplace tempted her over to heat water for her wash-down, and a most needed herb tea; a nerve-soother of oat-straw.

'Don't look at me like that. I do not want to leave this cosy nest'.

Curling up for what might have been another fifteen minutes, Elle finally gave into the need to start her day. Laughing at the fire, 'You win', she piled on more logs, grateful she was never short of heating, and placed a pot of water to boil. While she waited she wiped the window free from mist and peeked outside. Disappointment hit her and she sighed at the sight of the swirling fog. It rolled across the sea and moved on land its greyness cloaked the coastline. Just what she wanted, a mist covered landscape to trap her inside. Even the gull squeals were stifle and drifted on the fog; eerie, muffled sounds surrounded the cottage. Elle rubbed harder at the window in the hope of removing the fog with the palm of her hand.

Nothing. No view. How can I work with nothing to see? What an end to the year. Tomorrow will be 1866 the start of a brand new year. I wonder what it will bring for me.

After washing, she dressed and prepared food. Her kitchen looked homely with the new items she gradually introduced. Mrs Orris and Stanley often gifted her a small unused item they came across. It tickled Elle to think she owned more than her mother ever did. Memories of her Grandmother's home were of one full of colourful items in various places. Crammed corners of items that were considered useful or ornamental. Anything from an old magazine to a chipped pot, all offering a multitude of colour. Elle preferred more order to her small home, but wanted to fill it with bright things the same.

The weather showed no sign of improvement, a crosswind whipped across an angry sky, coming in from the north, layering sticky salt residue upon the windows. Resigned to a day indoors, Elle pulled out her artwork with the aim of drawing up a list of paint colours. After Christmas she started a small project of mixing the few paints she had to achieve more colours. Not wanting to waste time trying to remember the mixes, she made a smudge of each colour in a small book. Each shade was given a name. Nettle Green. Kale Green. Dead Crab Pink. Piglet pink. Sunset gold. Sunrise gold. Sand gold. Whelk brown. Angry sea grey and Sunny sea blue, were just some of her inventions.

A tap at the door was not followed by Stanley's entrance to the kitchen. Instead another tap made Elle realise this was another visitor. Not being used to people calling upon her, Elle panicked.

What if it is the owner of the property? Mayhap the old landlord had tracked me down!

'Who is it?' She called out, then chewed the edge of her thumb in anxious anticipation.

'Angus. Elle it is I; Angus.'

Elle pulled open the door expressing her surprise.

'Angus. What are you doing here? Is Stanley with you? Come in, that wind is evil today.'

'Thank you. I know it is improper of me to call unannounced, but-well-you are not a regular visitor to the shop, and I haven't seen Stanley to ask him. I would like to approach you for more of your work.'

'Sit. Please. Let me just put this away. I am blending my paints, as you showed me. Do you like Angus Gold?' Elle laughed as she held up a splodge of reddish gold, as red as his hair.

'I am honoured you should name me after your paints, my dear. Honoured indeed.' His laugh rang around the cottage.

'So, you want more of my drawings? How wonderful they sell as they do.'

'They are very popular, Elle. Especially with the visitors to town. Show me what else you have. Do you have any small paintings completed?'

Elle went to the wooden box where she stored her work and lifted out a thick pile.

'I have a few.' She giggled.

'My word, you have been busy. Let me have a look.' Angus laid the pile on the table and started browsing. He moved some to one side.

'They are good, but not to be sold just yet. Let's get the small ones sold first. The better ones we will charge more for, once you get a name for yourself. One lady has called in for another, making it a total of three she has purchased. She will be one I will tempt with one of your oils, but not yet. Hmm, there is a fine set of drawings here.'

He pulled one from the pile.

'This is an unusual one. Very unusual given the image. I have no wish to appear rude, but how do you know Charles Gant? He is one of the richest men in the area, and well…'

Elle sensed the blood drain from her face, her hands went cold and trembled. 'You know him?' She whispered.

Angus looked up at her and rushed over to her, guiding her to a seat.

'What on earth is the matter? You are ghostly. Here wrap this around you.' He rubbed her hands to give them warmth. Angus frowned.

'Did he hurt you? Elle, you can tell me the truth. I will keep your confidence.'

Elle shook her head. 'No. He didn't hurt me. Quite the opposite. He gave me a coin that got me home again.'

'Where did you meet him, and how on earth did you manage to draw him semi naked? Not something you should be exposed to at your age-artist or not.'

Elle indicated to the chair across the room. Angus sat and she relayed the story of how the drawing came about but not before she swore him to secrecy.

'The sly old dog. His wife would string him to the masts if she got wind of his antics. She is the moneyed one of the two. Without her he is nothing. Nothing.'

'She must never know. Poor woman, how dreadful for her to find out something such as that.' Elle started to pace the floor. 'Angus, this must go no further. Promise me you will not tell her.'

'Sit down. I promise. However, this little drawing is now worth a lot of money. Money that would set you on the right road. Do you realise how much he would probably pay to ensure he could destroy the evidence of his playtime?'

'You are not to approach him, Angus. The drawing can stay right here.

I cannot bring myself to destroy it, and besides when would you travel to Colchester to show him? You rarely leave town.'

'I don't have to travel anywhere. He is a customer of mine and lives locally. Let me take it, Elle. I promise he will be the only one to see it. I will tell him I came across it in a junk box. It will not involve you. The money will be useful, you must agree.'

Elle walked over and took the picture from him. Staring at it for a few moments, she handed it back.

'Take care of it, the charcoal could smudge if it is handle badly. I used some from the hotel room fire.'

Angus threw back his head and laughed. 'Elle you are a true artist. Never missing the opportunity for a willing subject. Except in his case it was an unknowing subject.'

'Do you really think he will pay? If he refuses, I will take it back. He must not be pestered into paying. Promise me, Angus. He did me no wrong.'

Angus patted her shoulder. 'I promise. I do know the man, and he will want to retain his reputation. I will be fair, Elle. Also, it is a decent piece of artwork and worth a coin or two.'

After Angus left Elle sat pondering the situation. Finally she decided not to fret over the drawing and to enjoy the money if it came her way. What she didn't want to come her way was the gent himself. No matter how hard she tried, she couldn't put the situation out of her mind, and at times regretted handing over the drawing to Angus.

***

The afternoon brought Stanley to her door. Elle had dragged around more driftwood to the side of the property and was brushing the mud from her clothing. She wore an old pair of his trousers for outside chores. Mrs. Orris had found her struggling in her skirts one day and sent a parcel of clothing more suited to the job. They saved her skirts from getting ruined. Especially when she climbed the roof to repair a slate or two.

'Have you been outside today? Not painting surely?' Stanley watched as she brushed out the clothing.

'Only for wood. The wind is too strong even for a quick sketch.' Elle folded away the clothes.

'Angus called by today. He took a few more pictures with him. Apparently my little drawings are becoming quite popular. The money earned is a blessing.

It feels good to be independent. How's your mother? Have you been to the quay? Can I get you a warm herb tea?'

Stanley grinned at her. 'She is well. Yes I have and yes please. Can you believe it is the end of the year?'

'I cannot but am relieved it is so. It has been the most dreadful year for me. My fresh start and wonderful new life is all I wish to focus upon from now on. This year I intend to travel on one of those new trains. What fun that should be. I am saving for a day out-to find new things to inspire me-will you come too?'

Stanley nodded as he sipped his tea. 'I hear they can take you as far as London in a matter of hours. Imagine.'

'I do not intend to travel so far. While I was painting a scene of Dovercourt beach, a gentleman stopped to look at my work. He mentioned an artist John Constable had painted the self-same scene years ago. I asked Angus about him, and he said if I go to Manningtree I can walk the fields to Flatford. There I will find the inspiration behind his paintings. That will be my destination in the spring.'

'London. That is where I would go. The capital City. I would visit the Queen and tell her of a rising young artist who wishes to paint her portrait.'

'Oh, wouldn't that be grand, Stanley. Queen Victoria in all her glory. Yes. I will come with you when you paint in London.'

'Well before you do that, Mother said you are to come to us for supper. And before you try to refuse, I was told not to return without you. Apparently Josh and his wife who work in the big house are going to be there, and Josh has said he will bring you home on the cart.'

'Who am I to argue with your mother? I will pack away my paints and get my cloak. We will leave in daylight and the fresh air will do me good. You know how I am when I am cooped up. I do hope tomorrow improves. How wonderful to paint on the dawn of a new year.'

CHAPTER 11

Fresh Roots

Elle pushed open the windows and let the fresh morning air flood into the room. A waft of cropped grass drifted upon the wind, and she inhaled deeply. Months of strong winter winds and rain now passed, and spring shared new growth. In the surrounding fields lush grasses, daffodils, wildflowers of many colours, and shadows from trees full of new life, gave a wonderful backdrop for new ideas.

The money Elle made from the sale of her hotel-room portrait had been wisely spent. The new owner had been more than willing to pay the artist one penny per week from the date of the drawing, plus a five pound lump sum. He also parted with a small fee for Angus. There had been no quibble on his account, his public standing depended upon their discreet, confidential agreement. They in turn promised to never reveal knowledge of the sketch.

Elle's words that day were that she felt she sold his dignity for a penny, Angus reminded her the money was food on her table, and would set her for life if spent wisely. With new equipment she could improve her skills.

With guidance from Angus, Elle purchased paints, brushes and a selection of canvases. Stanley made her pull along trolley stronger, and as a surprise, crafted her an easel from wood that lay around the farm. Elle could not wait to finish her present work, and start a new project. One last glance around the room she closed the door to the inside, and walked along the pathway, and embraced the outside with new vigour. She made her way to the area she had in mind for an ambitious project.

Propped upon a rock, she concentrated on the horizon. Shades of blue-grey trimmed with yellow-gold glistened below a soft, white clouded sky. Cloud shadows and a small red fishing smack bobbed around upon the gentle, silver-tipped waves. Seagulls called and played upon the breeze. Dipping in and out of the thermals.

Elle worked fast and furious, not wanting to miss a thing, the light was the best it had been for weeks. Colours invaded her mind, and their vivid calling made her hands fly across the page. She jotted notes with frantic pace. The pencilled etchings pulled together, and her vision came to life. A rough image but it satisfied the artist inside Elle.

Perfect. Perfect for my first full canvas.

After an hour she stood and stretched her limbs. Turning her back to the sea, she looked toward her little home. A small drizzle of smoke drifted upwards from the chimney and left its white trail rising toward the clouds. She spotted Stanley walking along the seafront. His limp not as prominent as during the colder months. Elle rose to her feet, and with great enthusiasm, waved her arms in the hope of catching his attention. Eventually he waved back and made his way over to her rock.

'Isn't it just the most beautiful morning, Stanley?' Elle looped her arm through his and they both looked out at the small boat still floating along on the soft surf.

'A most beautiful morning indeed, Elle. Even my legs appreciate the warmth. I could walk a little faster today. Oh, and the fishermen were in fine fettle. The catch baskets were full to overflowing. I left a box on the pathway beside your trolley, there will be a fish or two for your supper.'

Stanley eased himself onto a rock to her right, and sat in silence while she worked. When satisfied she had captured the scene, and nothing more could be added, Elle joined him. They sat in silence as she added a few finishing touches to her work. After packing away her things, she scuttled beside him and leaned her head on his shoulder. They had become comfortable in each other's company and all barriers were down. Both knew there was no romance between them, purely a strong, deep friendship. An outsider would have viewed the scene as more intimate than it really was.

'I am so lucky to have you as my friend, Stanley. You have given me new life. If my parents returned now, I could never leave with them. They are shallow, selfish people. I have no love for them. You and your mother, even in such a short time, have become my family. I have a fondness for you both. Love. Yes, I think it is a form of love.' Elle sighed and silence fell between them again. Stanley reached out and grasped her hand. He gave it a gentle squeeze in acknowledgement. He placed a gentle kiss on the crown of her head. Not the kiss of a lover, just a fleeting brush-kiss of a family member. A tingle of comfort winged its way to Elle's heart. Life gave her hope when Stanley was close.

'Time to get back to the path, the tide is turning. We will get cut off if one of these salt creeks fill, Elle. It is time to go home. And I too value our friendship. I too have a love for you, my little friend. We are a strange pair, you and I. Years apart in age, yet close in mind. A good friend I have found in you, I too am blessed. Mother and I had a conversation about the two of us only the other day. She was concerned about your reputation, but as I reminded her you mix with no-one, and there is no reason why my calling on you should tarnish you in any way. I explained how I felt about you. She decided our two souls were damaged and had found each other for repair. I am inclined to agree.'

'Your soul has definitely healed mine, Stanley.'

'And yours, mine, Elle. Now let's go and find you a decent size fish for supper.'

The wind rustled and gathered strength, yet remained calm. The gulls swooped and dipped around the friends as they watched the red boat turn back with the tide, and venture to the entrance of the quayside on its journey home. A crimson glow formed where the yellow-gold had once been, and the sun dropped low. The day was drawing to a close, and ready to give way to the early eve. The magic of the sea gave both Elle and Stanley a special moment in time. Both reluctant to leave it behind.

CHAPTER 12

Turning Tides

Elle followed behind her friend and marvelled at his ability to clamber over the rocks. His legs struggled on the slippery ones and she caught her breath each time he slipped. She shifted her canvas in her arms then glanced ahead to keep her balance.

In a flash of movement she watched Stanley lean to one side. In horror she saw him move as if in slow motion. Helpless, she watched him fall and his head appeared to bounce twice on the rock. She shook her own in disbelief. He slid into a crevice a few feet below. A pool of blood quickly formed and stained the sea as it ran down the pebbles.

'Stanley!' She screamed out his name and walked as swiftly to the shore as she dare. Placing her materials onto the bank she rolled up her skirt, tucked it into her waistband, and made her way back to Stanley. Clambering her way down to him her hands snatched at clumps of seaweed and stones embossed with limpets and sharp shells. Not caring about the pain to her own hands or legs, Elle focused on the figure below.

'Stanley. Can you hear me?' Elle panicked as the blood continued to flow. With one foot dangling in the water and the other underneath him, Elle could see Stanley had fallen at an awkward angle. Calling out for help was no good as there was not another person around for miles. Continuing her climb down, she heaved a sigh of relief when she finally reached him. She lifted his head from the water and wiped his hair away from his eyes. His face had a pallor to it and Elle could see no flicker from his eyes when she lifted his eyelids.

'No. This will not do Stanley, we have to move. The tide is rising. Stanley.' With a frantic scream of his name she tugged at his arm to no avail. He made no sign of movement.

Elle looked back at the sea, and the failing light around her clarified she did not have time to run to the farm for help. To leave Stanley would be leaving him to die in the tidal wash. She had no option but to save him herself. With gentle movements she rolled her friend onto his side. It was then she saw the deep gash where the sharp edge of the rock had penetrated. Thankful she was not squeamish, Elle wiped away what she could and eased her arms under his shoulders. Slowly she slid him from rock to rock, grimacing each time his limbs flopped hard against their edges. All energy was spent on getting him to shore, the tide started to lap over the large boulders and she was in danger of slipping over the edge. The seagulls screamed the screams she felt deep inside. At last she hauled him onto the embankment. With one quick decision she continued to drag him backwards to her cottage. There she would lay him on her bed and run for his mother. Thankful the light was still on their side, she settled him down and made good speed to the farm.

Mrs. Orris called for Josh to take them to the cottage on his cart. Elle agreed it would be easier for Stanley to be transported back in relative comfort, however every minute of waiting for Josh to hitch up the horse felt like hours. They stopped only to collect her trolley and the fish pail she had left on the pathway entrance.

After closer examination Stanley appeared warm but still unconscious. Not knowing what his condition was, or what could happen if they moved him again, they felt it best he stayed where he was and tend to him there.

Elle busied herself making hot tea, and relayed the accident between sips. Josh had placed a blanket from the cart around her shoulders when she began to shake and she felt comforted by the warmth. He also made her sip from his brandy flask.

'Josh, please fetch the doctor. I cannot stem the flow of blood. I think it best he is checked by a medical man.' Mrs. Orris rinsed bloodied rags as she spoke.

Josh left the cottage and the two women sat watching the man they loved. Elle trembled and did not stop the tears that fell.

'It's the shock dear.' Mrs. Orris comforted her. 'You did a brave thing going after him. Why you are only a scrap yourself. How on earth did you manage to get him here is beyond me.'

'If I hadn't been there in the first place, he wouldn't be lying there injured.'

'Nonsense child. Stanley knows his capabilities. He made the choice to join you. You know how he feels about you, and know well enough he was not out to impress you. If my boy wanted to sit and enjoy watching you paint, and knew he would endanger himself, he would not have attempted it. An accident, it was an accident and nothing more. Now calm yourself. The doctor will examine him and then we will know more about taking him home. The fall knocked him out cold and he will have one glorified head pain in the morning, mark my words.'

'Why Stanley though. He has been through enough.' Elle sobbed into her pinafore.

'No more tears. Sort his fish out, so he won't fret about them in the morning. Clean them and I will pickle a few tomorrow. Keep back some for yourself. I'll watch him. You keep busy and look out for the doctor. Each time Elle dipped her hands into the salted water her hands smarted and stung. She worked diligently through the pain, regarding it as her punishment for endangering her closest friend. She watched his mother and listened to her gentle crooning. How many times had the poor woman had to sit beside Stanley in the past? Life was not fair to the two kindest people she had ever encountered.

'How is he fairing?' She handed Mrs. Orris a mug of warmed milk and sat beside her.

'It is hard to tell, Elle. He shows no signs of waking.'

A sharp rap at the door startled them both. Elle leapt from her seat.

'That will be the doctor, Josh made good time.'

Josh and a tall willowy gentleman entered the room.

'Mrs. Orris, so sorry to hear young Stanley is in the wars again. Hmm, a blow to the head I understand. Josh, filled me in on the way here.' He turned to Elle. 'You must be Elle, Stanley's young lady.'

'Oh, gosh no, my Stanley took this little one under his wing. She is more a sister to him, certainly one of the family.' Stanley's mother interjected before Elle had chance to reply. She merely nodded at her friend's words.

The three stood back to allow the doctor room to examine Stanley. Elle chewed the edge of her thumb, Josh twisted his flat-cap and Mrs. Orris wrung the corner of her pinafore. Each one of them anxious to hear the outcome. Each time he muttered something inaudible, they glanced to one another for clarification, frowning in frustration.

At last the examination was complete and the doctor turned to face them.

'I must warn you, he is in a serious condition.'

Elle clutched hold of the table edge, Mrs. Orris sat down and Josh slipped outside to puff on his pipe.

'What are we to do, doctor?' Elle enquired.

'Leave him where he is, keep the room warm -as it is now, and hope. There is nothing more I can do, should he wake, offer him sips of warm fluids until morning. I will call again at first light.'

'Thank you doctor.' Mrs. Orris spoke in no more than a whisper. The doctor placed his hand on her shoulder as he was leaving. A gesture of comfort.

Elle instructed Josh to speak to the lady of the house after he had taken the doctor home. To inform her of the situation and the fact that Mrs. Orris would not be at work in the morning. Two hours later he returned.

'I spoke to madam and she asked me to inform you to take the time you need to see Stanley on his feet again. I have brought an extra chair, some blankets and food from your cottage Mrs O. The missus took the liberty of packing them for you and said not to worry about your fire, she will keep it stoked ready for when you bring the lad home. I am to fetch the doctor in the morning, so will see you then. I will bid you goodnight as I have a few chores left to do before I retire. Bless the boy and I hope all is well for the morrow.'

'Thank you, Josh. We will see you in the morning. It is going to be a long night.' Elle saw him out of the cottage and settled herself in a chair beside Stanley. Slowly the candlelight took over from the daylight and accompanied them into the early hours. The only sounds in the cottage were the gentle snores of Stanley's mother sitting slumped in the chair closest to his head. Exhaustion and anxiety had gotten the better of her. Elle on the other hand could not relax. Her eyes were fixed on Stanley for any sign of life. Silent prayers were sent skyward on her behalf and tears dropped intermittently while she waited.

A noise from the bed alerted both Elle and his mother that Stanley had some discomfort and both moved to his side.

'He has not woken. What is that noise?' Elle asked Mrs. Orris.

'A turn for the worse, I fear. It is his breathing, listen.' She put her fingers to her lips.

A harsh, rasping intake and expulsion of air came from Stanley's mouth. A dry choking sound.

'I recognise the sound from my father's illness. Pneumonia. His lungs couldn't perform properly. Feel his forehead, see? Hot and clammy. Fetch me a cool cloth, there's a girl. This is the end for my boy I fear.' A sob caught in her voice as she spoke.

Elle stared at Stanley transfixed to the spot for a few seconds, not certain of how to react. She wanted to shake his mother and tell her to stop thinking the worse.

'Elle, cold cloth. Now, please.' Mrs. Orris spoke in firm, slow manner and Elle shook herself out of her trance like state.

'He will be fine. Here, here's the cloth. What can I do?' She chewed on her thumb again, helpless would be how she would describe herself at that moment. Completely and utterly helpless.

'Pray, Elle. Pray to the Lord my boy will break his fever.'

Elle looked at her friend with his sweating brow and large blood-soaked bandage swathed around his head. She could not imagine life without him now, he was part of everything she did. In such a short period of time they had achieved a lifetime of friendship, and she dropped onto her knees at the bedside, placed her hands together and begged with a garbled prayer to whoever watched over Stanley to deliver him back in good health.

CHAPTER 13

Shades of Black

Shaking the hand of the last person leaving the cottage, Elle turned back inside. She picked up plates and dishes in an automatic fashion.

'How do you feel, girl?' Josh enquired.

Elle shook her head. 'Numb, Josh. I feel numb.'

'You ain't alone with that feeling, I can tell you.' He indicated with his head to where Stanley's mother sat. Her black mourning clothes made her features gaunter than the day Stanley died. Elle knelt by her side.

'Can I get you anything to eat? You haven't eaten for three days. Try something.' Despite the fact she herself had not eaten, she felt the need to encourage her friend to try.

'No thank you, Elle. Not today. In fact I think I shall retire. Thank you for being by my side, you have been of great comfort.' Mrs. Orris rose from her chair and kissed the top of Elle's brow. 'I might enjoy a warm herb tea later this evening. Your tea does me good. Get some rest yourself, it has been a hard day for all.'

Elle noticed how aged the woman had become. Her hair appeared streaked with more grey and her gait a slow amble, close to a shuffle.

'Sleep tight, and I will bring you tea at sunset. Josh has built up the fire in your room, so get some rest.' Elle looked to Josh. He stood shaking his head.

'Hit her hard. Poor woman done no harm in her life and now this. No justice I say. No justice. Ah, come girl, don't cry. Old Josh can't abide to see you in such distress. The boy is at peace now. And don't go blaming yourself all the time. I heard you telling old Smith you felt guilty. 'Twas an accident.' He nodded his head towards the door Stanley's mother had just walked out of. 'She will tell you, it was not your fault. The boy chose to climb them rocks. He led a normal life as best he can and made his own choices. Joining you out on the point was one of them. Get yourself some rest, we'll keep an eye on our friend. The wife made up a makeshift in the other room-not his room, the front parlour as they call it. You will be comfortable there. Tomorrow life will be different and things will need to be sorted. His things and some-such, she will need your help. Then you must be brave and return home. She will cope.'

'She might, Josh, but will I. How can I survive without him? He was my lifeline.'

'You will find a way, girl. For sure there is a plan for you somewhere. Now get that rest.' He guided her towards the parlour door. Elle climbed fully clothed onto the small truckle bed and fell into the first sleep she had experienced for days.

***

The following morning she kept herself busy by finding all items belonging to Stanley that were lying out of place. She piled them onto the table and folded those items that needed it. She held his jacket to her face and inhaled. A faint hint of fish and smoke still lingered. She hugged it to her breast.

Oh, Stanley, just when our broken souls had found each other, they are torn apart again. Come back to me, I beg you.

She continued clearing around the cottage and boiled water to take upstairs. It was too quiet and she thought it might be wise to rouse Mrs.

Orris and encourage her to start functioning again.

Tapping on the bedroom door, Elle received no response. She tapped again and this time entered. The room was sparsely furnished, but so pretty. The curtains hung in perfect pleats and matched the pink damask counterpane. A dressing table with delicate glass trinket holders sat against one wall, a large wardrobe against another and the bed faced the window. Carefully she laid the water jug into the large porcelain washbowl on the dresser. She pulled back the curtains to allow in what sunshine managed to struggle through.

Mrs. Orris lay curled asleep and Elle was reluctant to disturb her, however it would be now or never. She ventured under the bed for the chamber pot but found it unused. The fire had still retained a warm glow and needed no more logs. All chores in the room were done.

Feeling a little awkward she called out her friend's name, softly at first then remembering Rose was a little hard of hearing, she called a pitch higher. Gaining no response, she moved to the bed and gently shook the shoulder raised out of the covers.

'Rose. It is a new day. We have sunshine. Come now, it is time to rise.' Still she received no reply or noticed any movement.

With a cold clamped sensation in her chest, she pulled back the cover. Rose wore a pained, wide eyed expression and lay with her hands pressed against her ample bosom.

Elle recoiled. She regained composure and touched her face. It was cold. Rose had joined her son in death.

Collapsing onto her knees Elle sobbed into the counterpane until her legs and back objected. Slowly she moved closer and kissed the forehead of the woman who had shown her the love of a mother. She pulled the counterpane over the twisted face and left the room.

She found a young boy cleaning out the pigpen closest to the cottage, and gave him a message for Josh to fetch the doctor for Mrs. Orris. She made no mention of her death.

Within the hour the two men and Martha had arrived at the cottage. Elle told them of how she found Rose. Martha pulled her into her arms and held her while she sobbed. The doctor and Josh went to see Rose, they returned within minutes.

'She passed away due to a stroke. Her features are weak on one side and she has the indicative twist to her mouth. It does not surprise me. Her maladies were always connected with head pains. It was her time, the pressure of losing Stanley just became too much. Now young Elle, we have to ensure you stop this blaming of yourself about Stanley. Josh told me about your guilty feelings. Don't go blaming yourself about his mother. Rose Orris would have passed away sooner rather than later, and it is not, you hear me? Not your fault.'

Elle, unable to speak, nodded her head. His words whirring around but not registering inside. She would always feel guilty about Stanley and will never forget why her friend Rose died.

Josh saw the doctor out of the cottage, thanking him for his kindness and for refusing a fee.

'A good man that doctor. Not a penny would he take from her or us for this past week.'

Martha removed her arms from around Elle and for the first time since entering the cottage she spoke. Her tone gentle but firm enough to make Elle look up at her.

'Elle. We have a job to do, Rose was my friend and I want to attend to her,' she placed her hands on her hips and looked Elle in the face, 'Now I can get another woman from up the house, but-'

Elle cut her off, 'I'll help. Whatever it takes, I will help.'

'Good girl, it is only fitting after all. The woman saw you as a daughter. She may not have told you, but she told us, isn't that right, Josh?'

'Most definitely is, my love. She said it on more than one occasion. I must make way to the big house. I have to inform the master and his missus, and I know this sounds callus but I want to put in for the cottage. Ours is on the dull side over yonder and if I don't mention it today, I will lose my chance. Rose's cottage will be a better home for us don't you think, Martha?'

'I think yes, but do you not think it is a little out of turn to speak of such a thing now?' Martha's words sounded sharp and Elle looked between the two of them. Her new friends.

'Josh is right. If he says nothing then Rose and Stanley will be packed away in boxes. He must push for the cottage. It will bring me comfort to know you are cosy with her furnishings and his furniture carvings. Don't be angry, Martha. I understand.'

'For a little one you have a wise head. I suppose your circumstances have made you see things through different eyes. Well in that case, if we are successful you will be welcome to come live with us. Our home is your home, Elle.'

Elle stood staring out of the window into the sunlit yard, yet today she saw only shades of black.

'It is most kind of you, Martha, but I am of a mind to stay in my place while I can. I find inspiration from the sea for my paintings. Josh, you go and request the cottage. Martha, come we must attend to Rose. There is a lot to do today. Neither she nor Stanley would want us wallowing in tears and regret. We must move forward with our lives.'

Josh returned with the undertaker and Reverend Smith. Comforting words were offered and the funeral planned for the following day. Rose and Stanley would be buried together. The owner of the farm informed Josh he wished to visit in the afternoon. When informed of Elle, and of how she was to be included in their lives, he wanted the three of them to be in attendance.

'He wishes to speak to us about the future of this place, and I told him, you were important to Rose, and to us.

Please wait to hear what he has to say.' Josh relayed to Elle.

'Very well, Josh. However, as I said, I will remain where I am, and if you both could just keep where I live to yourselves, I would appreciate it. I am not sure how much of my background Stanley or Rose mentioned, but where I live might belong to someone, and I need to pay rent. Stanley couldn't find an owner so I remain there until I have to move. The fewer people know, the better. I trust you both, and if you would be so kind, should it arise, just mention I am moving to live with an aunt.'

'You can trust us, Elle. We will back your story. I do repeat our offer for you to remain living here.' Martha gave a smile, and Elle just nodded back in reply. No words were needed.

Both women set about various duties in the kitchen and Josh went back to his farm work. For Elle the day moved in a foggy haze of disbelief. One moment something would make her giggle, the next she was in tears as she replayed recent events in her mind. Martha was no different, they often comforted one another.

The afternoon arrived and with it the landowner. Elle busied herself at the sink and gave a backward glance greeting, with an apology for not being able to stop the task in hand. Martha played the hostess and offered him a seat and Josh stood waiting for a response to his morning request. The man discussed who Rose and Stanley had as family, and when it was established there was no claim on their belongings, he agreed to Josh and Martha having the cottage. After discussions that held no interest for Elle, the topic changed and he enquired more about her.

'Were you a ward of Mrs. Orris young lady?' he asked.

Elle turned to address the well-dressed man sipping a sherry offered by Martha. She could tell by his face it was probably on the sharp side, but nevertheless he had manners and continued sipping. He had a kind air about him. His features remained in the shadows, and Elle dried her hands before moving across the room to the small group.

'Not on paper sir. She and Stanley took me under their wing when my own family failed me. I never lived here, I-um-I-' She looked to the floor. To announce she lived in the old shepherd hut along the coastal path seemed like exposing herself to the outside world. 'I lived in Parkeston, but moved to lodgings close by when my parents passed.' Elle had no qualms about using the word passed in relation to her parents. For her they had passed her by, for others it hinted they had died. In her heart she considered they had done the latter.

'I am sorry to hear you have experienced more loss in your life. As for where you live, your secret is safe with me.' The man took a sip of the drink he held, and gave a slight cough.

Meanwhile, Elle looked to Josh and Martha, both of who shook their heads in denial of telling.

'You know where I live? Is it yours sir? Do I owe you rent? Only Stanley said he couldn't find the owner and…'her words tumbled over themselves as she spoke.

The man stood up and moved to face her. He smiled and Elle could not help smiling back at him. There was something familiar about his eyes as the skin crinkled around them. Finally it dawned on her and a mix of fear and panic sped through her veins, and she dropped her head to stare at the floor, remembering when she did the same once before in his presence.

The man in the hotel room. It's the man who bought my drawing. Oh, it's all too much.

'Calm down young lady. Stanley was a good man. A kind hearted soul. You obviously do not know he owns the cottage, I gifted it to him before his accident. It was run down and he approached me about fixing it up to live in, he offered a small price. There was a young woman who had caught his eye and he wanted to make a home from the place. I had no use for it, the land it sits on is only a square of nothing, so I drew up papers to complete the gift. I did not need his money. I told him he could work off the price by making me a piece of furniture, which incidentally is my pride and joy in my study. Legally when I die, it would transfer to him, but in the meantime it would be his to do whatever he wished. Sadly, his accident meant he could not repair the place and the girl found another heart to break elsewhere. I offered to have my men work on it, but Stanley refused. He remained with his mother. The cottage, in some manner, belongs to Stanley Orris and myself. However, so far as I am concerned, the place is part of his affairs not mine. He never found the landlord because it was he who would have claimed rent from you. As I understand it you were very close friends. Were you to marry?'

Elle listened to the words in wonderment. Stanley owned the cottage. He'd loved a young woman?

'No sir. We were good friends but nothing beyond that. The Orris's were more family than friends. There was no romance between us, merely a brother, sister relationship. Stanley helped me during a very bad time in my life. I owe him more than I can say. What will happen now-with the cottage? Who owns it now? Thanks to Angus Argyle I can afford a small rent. But who will I pay it to?'

The man gave her a strange look, Elle prayed inwardly that he had not recognised her from the hotel. Then it dawned on her, she had mentioned Angus. Hoping the man never put the two things together and added her into the equation, she stood waiting for an answer.

'Sir? Who do I pay in order to live in the cottage?' She asked again. His silence unnerved her. Josh and Martha sat with quizzical looks upon their faces, they too must have seen a change in his manner.

'You know Angus Argyle the artist? How do you know him? What exactly is it you do for a living Miss Buchanan?'

His tone was cautious, as if he already knew what her reply would be, and Elle took a deep breath before she replied. She brought herself to full height.

'I am an artist sir. I know Angus through my work. He buys my drawings at a very good price. Thanks to him, I earn a decent living. I recently sold one at a very good price, a keen buyer so I am told.'

Realisation of what she told him flickered across the face of the man she had seen naked. Bewilderment and anxiety stared back at her. Elle stared him in the eye, willing him to understand their secret was safe. The man cleared his throat.

'In light of the present situation, the cottage officially still belongs to me. I can destroy the paperwork with no legal issue. My feelings are that should he have lived to a ripe old age, and I passed, Stanley would have wanted you to remain living there. So I am of a mind to gift it to you. This time I will do it legally and have my men fence off the official area. They will repair it to a good standard. You will own the deeds, Miss Buchanan.'

Elle stared open mouthed. Josh and Martha sat shaking their heads, wide smiles across their faces.

'Sir, I cannot accept such a gift, I have not earned the right of ownership.'

The man held out his hand.

'My name is Charles Gant, I am the owner of so much land this one small gift is no more than a pimple on a horse's backside.'

Martha sucked in a mouthful of air as a gesture of distaste to his choice of comparison. He chuckled and turned to her.

'Forgive me. I forget myself at times. You have heard me make my offer, now all you need is to persuade this young woman to accept it, I will leave the offer open for another two days. Today has been hard on you all and now is not the time for business transactions. I will of course attend the funeral with my wife. Do not worry yourselves with baking foods, I will have cook send down a selection for the wake. Rose was a good woman, and we were lucky to have her work for us. Thank you for the sherry, Josh I need to speak to you about assisting the Jacobs into your place. It will be a better cottage for him, as I hear he is to become a father soon. Martha, my wife will need to replace Rose. Who better than you? You have assisted her for many years and know the ropes. Neither Stanley nor Rose's deaths will have been in vain. Miss Buchanan …'

'Elle, my name is Elle sir, and I will accept your kind offer. I do not need two days to ponder over such generosity, if the place meant so much to Stanley, I shall keep it going. Only a fool would turn down such a gift. Although I will consider it a gift from Stanley, and not yourself if you don't mind.' She stared at the man, indicating she would not take a bribe to keep quiet about his private activities. He nodded and she could see he fully understood her meaning.

'But of course, I would not wish it any other way. I do have one request of you. I would like a portrait of my wife for the main hall and should like to commission you for the task. Argyle painted me many moons ago, but my wife might benefit from the softer eye of a woman. What do you say?'

Elle held out her hand. 'I would like that very much. A portrait would be challenging my capabilities, but I feel sure I can paint something that pleases the eye, with daring she ventured further, I have done so in the past, and never miss the opportunity of a worthy model. Thank you for the opportunity.'

Charles Gant flushed, and Elle allowed a soft smile play on her lips. He gave a nod of his head had left, the three friends were left staring at each other. It was Josh who broke their silence.

'Well I never did. What a day for mixed up affairs,' He banged his cap against his thigh, 'We all have a new roof over our heads, new jobs and found out our Stanley was a secret landlord. Rose must have known all along.'

Elle sat at the table, Martha handed her a small glass of sherry, but she shook her head.

'No thank you. I saw my mother drink one too many. Can you believe in a few days I will own a cottage by the sea? In so few months I have laid starving in Colchester, met friends, cried over their deaths, sold my drawings and become a property owner. My mind is spinning with it all.'

Martha wiped her hands on her pinafore. 'My palms are damp with having my hands clenched. I have fought back tears of joy for fear the tears for dear Rose would fall, and I would not be able to prevent them. What a day, and tomorrow we have to face more emotional upheaval. I suggest we eat a hearty supper and get some rest. Elle, you will stay here the night, as you did last. Josh and I will return home for a few personal items. We will sleep in the kitchen so you are not alone. I cannot sleep in her room just yet.'

CHAPTER 14

Fulfilling Dreams

April ventured into the world on a soft breeze, bringing with it perfumes of new hope.

The day arrived to move back home and Martha reprimanded Elle for eating her morning meal at a breakneck speed. Josh hitched up the cart and loaded her personal belongings, plus many new items that had belonged to Rose and Martha. She was also given a carved wooden travel chest made by Stanley. Inside were linens and items of a practical nature.

Upon her arrival home Elle noted the wooden fencing and newly planted garden surrounding a freshly plastered and roofed cottage. With squeals of delight she had jumped from the cart which again, earned her a ticking off from Martha. As she ran towards the small gate she left behind words such as, "unladylike behaviour" and "dangerous". She didn't care, her dream home lay before her.

Charles Gant and Angus waited by the front door. Angus waved on her approach and Charles smiled and nodded. It was a moment of mixed feelings. Elle refrained from running from room to room, and allowed herself to be given a guided tour. Her kitchen had new fittings and fire surround, and the small store room had been transformed into a pantry. The cook from the Gant family home had stacked each new shelf with so much foodstuffs, Elle declared she would not need to purchase another item for a year. Her bedroom housed a new bed with ornate carvings on each corner of the bedstead. The bedding was thick and luxurious in a deep shade of crimson edged in gold. Elle was immediately transported back to the day in room eighteen and sensed her cheeks burning. She glanced sideways at Charles Gant who to her surprise gave a knowing grin. Another thank you for keeping quiet about the whole embarrassing affair.

Angus, like Elle could hardly contain himself when they entered the main room of the house. Although he had seen it built, he had not seen it completed. Light flooded in from the large window dressed only with fine lace drapes pulled to one side, and the pale lemon walls glowed. Along another side of the room, a large easel stood with various packages stacked upon a long bench. A large table and four chairs furnished one corner and two large comfortable high backed armchairs sat either side of a fire place. Above the mantle in pride of place was a framed image. One which prompted a flow of tears from Elle. It was the portrait drawing she had done of Stanley. Angus explained that Martha had found it amongst his belongings and mentioned it to Charles. He in turn approached Angus, who framed it in an ornate, walnut frame.

'We thought this would be the ideal place to hang his portrait, Elle.' Angus explained. 'If it is too soon or upsetting for you, we can remove it.'

Elle moved closer to the picture and stroked the smooth wood. 'No. Leave it. This is his home too, he will be a comfort to me during my dark days.'

'I have registered the cottage in your name, and there is one form to sign. Angus has agreed to be witness.'

The sat at the large table and Elle trembled with excitement when she signed her name.

'So now Miss Elle Alice Buchanan, you are the proud owner of Orris Cottage.'

'Thank you, Mr. Gant. It was a pleasant touch naming the cottage after the Orris family. It is all so much to take in, I cannot believe my good fortune. Thank you again for all this.' She swept her arm in a circular movement around the room.

'Speak nothing of it. We both know the reason I have supported you. This is the last time you will thank me.' Charles Gant turned to look out to sea. 'Just make something of yourself with that talent of yours. My wife will be expecting you Monday next, as arranged. Goodness knows this portrait had better be worth the money she has spent on clothing and jewellery to wear.'

'The lassie has a keen eye as we know, she will make a grand job. I hope to be invited to the unveiling, Charles?' Angus gave a small wink at Elle. She watched the back of Charles Gant's head, his ears glowed a rose red. She wondered what shade his face might be. Angus had touched a nerve. She made light of the enquiry.

'Oh, it will not be worthy of an unveiling, Angus. Mrs Gant will be portrayed in the best light, and I am certain both will be pleased. No fuss need be made. I will see you out, Josh has offered to take you back to Harwich. He is fetching fish, now...' Her voice trailed off and she glanced up at

Stanley remembering their first meeting and her crab supper, 'now Stanley is no longer here to supply us with our fish, Josh fetches it.'

Charles Gant turned back to face them, his colour a natural shade of pale tan. 'I must make way and will bid you goodbye. No doubt our paths will cross from time to time, and I wish you well.' He lifted her hand and kissed the back of it. Elle felt embarrassed at his gesture. He treated her as a lady and she lowered her gaze.

'Thank you again for securing my future. I am most grateful sir.'

'As I said before, no more thank you speeches. Now kindly see me out of this establishment.' Charles Gant gave such a hearty laugh it made Elle jump.

After everyone had taken their leave, Elle unpacked the various items she brought with her. Rose's plates were passed onto her by Martha, and Josh had already put the holders in place. She stood on chair and carefully put each one on show. Stanley's trunk was emptied and she dragged it into the main room. She could not bear the thought of it sitting hidden in her bedroom and moved it into her painting area. All art materials were stored inside and she stood back looking at it with pleasure.

'So Stanley. I own a cottage with your name attached. My you were quiet about that, and the girl in your life. I wonder who she was and shame on her for breaking your heart. Can you see the glorious view from there?' Elle chatted along while she placed her table linen and few pieces of tableware into a small cabinet beside the table. 'What a home we have now. Fit for a queen. The wood stack outside is to the roof and I have two barrels of water. Mr. Gant has arranged for a regular barrel to be delivered when his is brought to town. Brackish water has leaked through his pipes, so he has it brought in on a regular basis. Can you believe it? My small drawing was worth more than I ever dreamed of. Oh, by the by, Angus and I are taking a trip to Manningtree. We are heading off to visit Flatford as I mentioned. I do wish you could have joined us. Who knows mayhap you will. Do try Stanley. Do try.'

Elle found talking to Stanley's portrait gave her the comfort she sought. He and Rose had left a large void in her heart, and if she could exchange all she now owned to have them back she would without blinking an eye.

'We'd had such a perfect moment that day, Stanley. I will never forget it and will remember your words for the rest of my life. I promise you this; I will follow our dreams. One day I will paint in London.'

CHAPTER 15
Spiteful Assumptions

A last glance in her artist trolley reassured Elle she had everything required for her visit to the Gant home. Today she was to start on the portrait of Evangeline Gant. Charles warned her his wife did not own a glowing personality, and he also warned Elle not to rise to anything the woman said, she had a twisted mind, and evil tongue. It had crossed Elle's mind as to why he married her, then she recalled Angus mentioning it was for money.

With improvement in the weather, Elle told Charles she did not need the transport he offered. Giving herself plenty of time, she took a slow walk dragging the tools of her trade behind her. Josh had suggested she invest in a pony and trap of her own, but Elle had laughed.

'I am only just coming to terms with owning a house. To ride around in my own trap would seem far too above my station, Josh.' He had disagreed with a shrug of his shoulders.

Elle knew no matter where her life took her, the trolley she pulled would be by her side. It had been part of her survival kit, and her friendship to Stanley when he repaired it for her. Never could she part with such a memory piece.

Spring lambs skittered around the fields below the big house as April gave way to a perfumed, May. A warm, friendly building with many windows and engraved features surrounding them. Wild flowers, succulent fresh grass blades, and rose bushes bloomed and budded along the long elegant pathway, their fragrance swirled amongst that of the farmyard aroma below. Sounds of whistles and timid bleats joined in with the song of birds in surrounding trees. All visual treats gifted with aroma and sound inspired Elle to form images in her mind. She stopped to smell a rose.

What a day to have to sit inside. I wonder if Mrs Gant would like her portrait etched outside in the grounds.

Her instructions had been to go to the kitchen door where she would be shown into the drawing room. A room which, Elle found to her frustration, was draped in dark coloured, heavy materials. All light was blocked from entering through the small square-paned windows she could just about see through gaps in the curtains. Her fingers itched to pull them back and push open the large doors that obviously housed them. She tried to focus on the decorations adorning every table and ledge in the room. The sense of claustrophobia increased with every moment she stood waiting for her model. Her foot tapped impatiently, when at last the door was pushed open with such force, Elle stumbled backwards and knocked her hip on the corner of a unit nearby.

A tall, thin woman swept into the room dressed in a large, satin gown in a dark green. Her pale features were not enhanced by her greying hair pulled back tightly into a large bow draped down the back of her neck. The woman stared at Elle through what she could only describe as spiteful eyes. Cold, staring and slit with suspicion.

'So you are the little witch my husband claims can paint. Amused him in his bed did you? Of course. Why else would he fancy up a cottage for you. A love nest by the sea.' Her tongue, as mean as her eyes, whipped out insults while Elle stood silently with her head held high. She waited for the onslaught of words to finish and drew in a deep breath.

'Madam, I am here at the request of your husband. For your information, the cottage was bequeathed to me upon Stanley Orris's death,' Elle took another deep breath and spoke before the other woman had chance. 'Although, Madam, my personal life is not the business of others, I will confide I have lain with no man in my life, and most certainly not your husband. My name is Elle Buchanan, I am not a witch and I can see my presence causes you some distress, so I will take my leave. Good day to you, Mrs Gant.' Elle walked to the door and brushed by the woman who had paled even more and looked at her in disbelief.

'Wait where you are. How dare you speak to me in that manner? You are here to paint my portrait, something I wish to be carried out. Angus Argyle is a fool and I dislike his heathen attitude. I am surrounded by fools, and may as well endure another. We will begin the work and I wish to be seated by the window over there. I will sit upon my father's chair, the large brown one in the corner. Do not delay me any longer.'

Elle parted her lips ready to quip back she was not part of the working staff. She refrained from doing so, and reminded herself this woman was a stepping stone into the world of art.

'Very well. Shall I ring the bell for someone to assist you with moving the furniture?' One thing Elle was not going to do was to allow the woman to treat her as a servant.

'Pardon?' Evangeline Gant squeezed her thin lips into a straight line, until it was hard to define the top and bottom. Both nostrils pinched into white tips. Spite written across the face of nastiness. Elle again drew herself upright, and kept her hand hovering over the pull rope. 'Yes. Yes. Time is of the essence. I am a busy woman and have better things to do than sit around having my portrait painted. My foolish husband insists.' Elle pulled the rope and watched the older woman preen herself in the mirror.

How on earth could Charles Gant be married to this cold fish of a woman? Vain too. Her husband insists? She wants the portrait, he certainly does not. If ever there was a witch in the room—

While they waited for the furniture to be moved into the satisfactory spot, Elle set out her drawing pad and pencil. Persuading Evangeline Gant to sit more in the light than the shade had proved fruitless so she made do with using her imagination more than her visual skills.

CHAPTER 16
Unwelcome Gestures

'Good day, Miss Buchanan. I see you are busy with something more attractive today.'

The male voice behind her made Elle freeze mid brush-stroke. She recognised the voice of Matthew Gant and did not appreciate the closeness of it to her right ear. She sat without comment still facing the sea. Inhaling, she continued on with painting seagulls lazily drifting on the pathway of a gentle easterly breeze. Again the voice interrupted her flow, and this time brought with it a soft warm waft of breath. Sweet breath, mead wine breath.

Nerves twitched in her arm and she laid down her brush. His closeness to her body was offensive and worrisome. She had encountered inebriated men before but had been able to move away into a crowd. This time she was alone and not certain if he had imbibed in too much, or just enough.

'Sir, I fear you are blocking my light. Would you mind stepping to one side, please?' She felt diplomacy would help rather than crying out with indignation.

Matthew Gant laughed and she heard the crunch of his boots as he moved aside.

'The maid needs good light and shall have good light.' His mocking tone was too much, and Elle stood up from the rocks and faced him with her hands on her hips.

'I sir, am no maid. Nor am I in need of company, so if you wish to continue your walk, I suggest a cool dip in Bobbit's Hole.'

Again the laugh rang around the cliff edge and echoed through hollow caverns.

'My dear, Miss Buchanan. I apologise for my torment. Please, can we set our friendship upon a different path?' Matthew Gant held out his hand, but Elle had no desire to shake it while she was disadvantaged. She grabbed her hand cloth, and wiped her hands over and over.

'Sir, you have no wish to shake my hands today. They are tacky with oils and I fear they will mark your fine, kid gloves. Forgive me, if you have no intentions of moving on, then I will consider my day finished. I do have your mother's portrait to complete.'

'Ah, mother's portrait. How can you bear to look upon that scowling hag and find any inspiration to put to canvas? How? Pray tell.' He sat upon a dry boulder and crossed one leg over the other. Elle could not help but admire the bulge of his thigh through his britches. He was a fine specimen of a man, and new sensations swept over her, ones she needed to shake and focus upon the man he really was, a wastrel, cad, and any other named good-for-nothing with money. Flustered she looked to the floor but the perfect curve of his calf in his leather boots warmed her cheeks. Matthew Gant formed a perfect body and it disturbed her insides in a way she could never describe.

'What a dreadful thing to say about one's mother. She has fine features.' Elle flounced around packing up her materials. She needed to rid her mind of the pictures flashing to the forefront. Images of her hand upon his thigh, of his upon hers. She shook her head and packed with dramatic flair and thought about his mother, that woman cleared all pleasant thoughts from any mind. What he had said was so close to the truth she dared not let him see it in her face. His mother was not an attractive woman, nor would she make a handsome male. The term hag suited her. Before she had the opportunity to voice any opinion, he threw back his head, revealing a slim, muscular throat, and again, Elle needed to refocus on his words.

'Come now, even your artistic eye cannot find beauty in her flesh, nor in her words. She is a spiteful, bitter woman. Her money is the only thing that becomes her. Sadly, I am not to benefit. It appears I have been a bad boy and am out of favour with dear mama. Your friend and his father saw to that.' He swiped his horse whip against the boulder and the sharp slap rang out, it sent shivers through Elle. She feared he might become agitated. She used a soothing, understanding tone, when in reality she wished to berate the idle, arrogant fool before her, and remind him of the harm he created in Stanley's life.

'A tragic event so I am told. I am certain you have made amends for the accident over and over. Stanley and his mother are now at rest, old wounds need not be re-opened. Time will heal the rift between you and your mother. You are fortunate to have one around you on a daily basis.'

'I understand you live alone. My father's prodigy so I am told. Sly old dog is dear papa.' His words anger Elle, and she now wanted rid of the drunk before her.

'You have been told wrong I am afraid. If I am to be branded the prodigy of any man it will be that of Angus Argyle. He set me on the road of painting, he mentors me in the art world, no more than that, before your guttered mind decides otherwise. With regard to your father, as I told your mother, the cottage was repaired because of an agreement between him and Stanley, prior to Stanley's death. Upon my inheritance your father felt it his duty to put right what he had promised.' Elle again used the agreed story between her and Charles Gant. A man she felt sorry for on a daily basis. With a bored, drunk of a son and an ice-maiden for a wife, it was little wonder he sought the warmth of another elsewhere.

'A thousand pardons madam for offending you.' Matthew retorted in a sarcastic tone. Elle began her walk home without responding. She had become bored of his company. Good looks did not make him a gentleman.

She pulled her trolley along the bumpy ground, and each bump rattled jars and brushes. Fearing her canvas would be damaged she stopped to rearrange the box on wheels. A shadow cast over her, and once again Matthew Gant blocked light but this time he also blocked her right of way.

'What a pathetic contraption. For all your airs and graces, you wander along the coastline in rags, and pull a child's toy full of paraphernalia behind you. Have you any concept of how you look? You are a wasted beauty. You should be in London, mixing with the rich. Any man would throw money at you to make you their wife. And yet you prefer to live hermit like with your head in the clouds, selling little drawings to feather-headed females who have never seen true artists at work. Paris, I should take you to Paris and show you real artists at work. Harwich is no place for you.' He kicked around a pebble on the pathway and tapped his whip as he spoke.

Elle stood still, mouth agape at his speech. When her words flowed they did so with a louder tone than she would normally use, and with as much bite as his mother would deliver.

'My *toy* for your information, was made for me by my father, who is no longer with me. It was repaired by my friend, who also is no longer with me. It is full of memories and *paraphernalia* that assist me in putting food on my table. I do not have the benefit of rich parents, I need to earn my food. Paris, London or any city in the world has no appeal to me. Harwich has a raw beauty of its own, and I intend to capture it on canvas for whichever *feather-headed female* wishes to purchase and hang in their home. Now forgive me, despite my lack of breeding, I have no desire to be delayed by a gentleman with the manners of a gutter rat. Good day to you.'

'My, my, the fine filly has a temper. I like a woman with fire in her bones. Forgive my banter, Miss Buchanan. I will let you go…,' he bowed, and left two words hanging in the air, 'for today.'

Elle felt him push his body into her as he moved past. Remaining rigid until he had passed, she eventually let out a breath she hadn't realised she was holding.

The nerve of the man. How dare he treat me like a street whore. A man to be avoided.

She waited until she could no longer see him, just a dot in the distance and made her way back to her home. The day had started out so well, but turned sour the moment he arrived. Elle sensed a change in her mood and knew it would be wrong to start working on the Gant canvas. She stored away her work and chatted to Stanley's image as naturally as if he was standing in the room. She painted wild flowers growing along the coastline. A simple project to help calm her jangled nerves.

'And the audacity of the man to treat me so badly. Not once did I fear you or feel uncomfortable in your presence, but he makes my skin tingle with nerves. I aim to steer clear of that one. He has his father's looks and his mother's cold streak, a dangerous combination.'

'Who are you talking to might I ask? Who has a dangerous combination? Tell me, do.' The male voice startled Elle and her brushes clattered to the floor. Leaning against the door jamb of the large glass doors overlooking the sea, stood Matthew Gant. Light played around his head and Elle noticed an ironic circle of light above his head. He was the last person to have the right to wear a halo, she stored the image away for future sketching.

'Don't move. Do not enter my home. How dare you enter my property without my permission?!' Elle bent to retrieve a stray brush from under a chair. When she stood up, Matthew Gant was standing beside her. His breath sweet with fresh clove, his hair shone with pomade oils, and his facial hair trimmed to perfection. Since their previous meeting he obviously felt the need for a grooming session. Elle, conscious of her unruly hair sitting upon her shoulders, swept her hands upwards and made a half-hearted effort to tidy herself. For a reason she could not think of, her heart gave a double beat.

'Mr. Gant. You startled me.'

'I came to apologise for my boorish behaviour back there.' He flicked his head in the direction of where she had been painting at their last meeting.

'Sir, your apology is dutifully accepted. I request you now please leave.' Not sure on who she was trying to convince, she added, 'You are not welcome here.'

He stepped over the threshold. A smile flittered across his face, light danced around him as if in celebration of his arrival. She wanted to paint the moment, to capture his handsome features.

Gain control, Elle. What is wrong with you?

Elle stood and stared past his shoulder, straightened her own and pointed outside. 'I asked you not to enter my home, and you have ignored my request. For the last time I ask that you leave.' Throwing aside the brush,

Elle advanced towards Matthew, and pushed into his chest. He snatched hold of her hand and drew him into his body. He moved his head sideways and moved his face into hers. His intention was clear. Elle twisted her head out of reach so his lips kissed only her hair. He overcorrected her face with a soft hand, and his warm lips found hers, Elle gave into the kiss, her first true embrace. Her head swam with so many new vibrations and sensations it took her breath away. His hand cupped her face and he pulled back with a softness in his eyes. Astounded by the moment, Elle stared back at gentle creases that surrounded eyes full of genuine surprise, and flushed lips burned with pleasure, glistened with moisture, widened with a satisfied, simple smile, but she saw no sign of the boorish male she encountered earlier in the day. His eyes settled a warm tingle across her body and he tilted her chin, then once more he cupped her face with gentle hands.

Elle, nervous of how much she enjoyed the first kiss, and of how attracted to Matthew Gant's physique she had become, pulled her face from his warm palms. Although she ached for another, Elle knew she should not encourage a second kiss. She struggled to compose herself and attempted an air of indignant expression.

'How dare you. Go. Out. Your father will hear of this behaviour. Who do you think you are sir?' Again she pushed into his chest and he took a step backwards. As if in slow motion Elle watched as he stumbled over the lip of the step and fell onto his back, fortunately hitting the soft ground, and missing the rose bushes nearby.

The tension she felt slid away, he looked so comical and undignified, she let slip a giggle, which as he struggled to his feet became a loud laugh.

'You think it funny, Miss Buchanan?' He stepped towards her.

'Most entertaining, Mr. Gant. Most entertaining. Now please forgive me, I am extremely busy. Good afternoon.' Elle closed the doors behind her and waited to see what he would do next. With relief she watched him walk away.

'Well Stanley, what do you think about that little episode? How dare he treat me so? Let us hope his dignity is not too bruised, and he finds another female to dally with.' She ran her fingers across her lips, and reflected upon when they enjoyed a new, pleasurable experience. Then she fancied she heard Rose and Stanley reprimanding her, and she dismissed the magic of the moment within seconds.

Shake out of it, Elle Buchanan. He is not for the likes of you. A danger to you, that is what he is, a danger.

Elle spent the rest of the day preparing for her visit to Flatford with Angus the following morning, and every now and then gave a giggle when she thought about Matthew Gant's fall from grace. She packed a small valise with artist materials, and planned a picnic. Travelling on the train was something to be experienced by all, according to Angus, and Elle hoped she would be as enthusiastic after their trip. Her stomach fluttered nervously whenever she thought about climbing upon the speeding machine. Another new chapter in her whirlwind life. For a fleeting moment she wondered if her parents had experience the latest form of travel. A hint of sadness threatened to move inside her heart, and she opted to shut the door to it, and removed the thoughts from her mind. She grabbed a pencil and scribbled a comical sketch of her visitor sitting upon the floor. Her art always filled the hole in the space where her parents should reside inside her heart. Art was her focus; her life.

CHAPTER 17

Eyes Wide Open

Angus ushered Elle through the entrance gate and onto the station platform. What appeared to be a whole town of people milled around, and Elle noted with interest the different classes by their clothing.

Navvy gangs moved industriously, clearing and cleaning. A moustached gent in a smart black suit with gold buttons, stood nearby with a red flag by his side, and Angus informed her he was the station master. Large carts of postal sacks and a stack of different shaped goods sat by the platform edge. Parcels and passengers waited patiently to start their journey upon the large steam vehicle approaching. It crept in slowly but certainly not quietly, gushing out large plumes of black smoke. Women in gowns to envy, fanned themselves against the smoky atmosphere.

Elle put her gloved hands to her ears as the loud whistle sounded, and the gush of steam screamed its way through the brakes while the machine ground to a halt.

'Magnificent beast, don't you think, Elle?' Angus shouted as he nudged her forward to a carriage doorway.

'You first, Angus. Please.' Elle heard the anxious words squeak from her throat. Her nerves would not allow her to climb on board for fear the beast would move off with her alone, and never return.

With great enthusiasm, Angus leapt onto the slim step and once balanced in the carriage he held out his hand to assist her.

'Come along. Take courage, Elle, it is perfectly safe. I promise.' She clutched his hand and lifted her skirts, found the step and climbed into the carriage. They sat on the wooden benches and looked back out onto the platform. Elle watched the goods being loaded into large carriages.

'It is quite an incredible thing, the railway. The speed in which it can deliver goods to London has made a difference to the fishing sales so I understand.'

Angus nodded in agreement, 'Made a difference to many things. Jobs for many from far and wide. You will see the small shacks along the way. They belong to the men drafted in to build the lines. They enjoy an ale or two, I can tell you. Shocking fights ensue some evenings near my home.'

With a shudder and splutter the engine pulled away on the sound of the whistle. Again Elle covered her ears and Angus laughed. The countryside sped past them as they headed towards their destination. Field upon field rolled by and Elle clutched to the edge of her seat for fear of falling off, much to Angus' amusement.

'Relax, Elle. Enjoy the view. Look, there is Mistley. We are nearly there. Please; relax.'

Elle smiled at him, he was so excited and she felt dreadful for being such a bore. He switched his head from one side to another taking in the scenes before them. Elle dare not do the same too often as the movement of the carriage created a mild nausea. At last the train eased into a slower pace.

'Manningtree. We are here, time to dismount.' Angus jumped to his feet and lurched sideways into an empty bench opposite.

'For all that is good, Angus, please keep seated until we have stopped. You will break a limb.' Elle watched other passengers rise from their seats but she remained firmly in position until the juddering eased.

'Now the adventure begins. Come, Elle. No time to dally.' Angus assisted her out of the carriage and they walked the length of the platform, jostling through the excited crowd. Grateful to be away from the snorting beast and throng of people talking at different levels of loud, she kept pace with Angus as he headed toward the field beside the station. The weather was ideal for walking and just as well, for Angus informed her they had several fields to get through before they arrived at their final destination. Elle had never seen or heard him so animated and his enthusiasm was intoxicating. Her heart pumped with excitement more than from exertion.

'Flatford was a great favourite of Constable. He painted many scenes, and I can see why. I dare you not to fall in love with what I am to show you today.' Angus kept up a running commentary of what surrounded them, and of how to interpret images onto canvas using different strokes of a brush, and shadowing the way Constable used his talent. Elle listened intently, her lessons about the local artist were her favourite, and her excitement about seeing where he painted overrode the fear of the train. She knew if she had given into her fear, she would never see through John Constable's eyes.

Already she absorbed the colours and shadows, tucking away ideas in her busy, creative mind. Angus marched on a mission of intent, and she stumbled a few times trying to keep up with him. Each time she stumbled Elle took a moment to take in the view, and Angus would call back to her to move ahead before the light lost its glory, the best was yet to come. Stile after stile they clambered and strode along the Cattawade marshes until the water mill came into view. Angus hurriedly sketched a horse-drawn lighter being guided down the river by a youth. The barge-like boat, laden with cargo, bobbed stoically along its journey. Time ticked in rhythm with daylight, and soon the afternoon ambled along in a leisurely fashion. Elle enjoyed the slower pace of the day -apart from the speeding train. She was still unconvinced it was a pleasurable, safe way to travel - and both she and Angus took in the delights of Flatford with an enthusiasm only another artist could appreciate. They sat in silence, and Elle continued to note the variety of colours and textures around her. For over an hour the artist in her sketched small drawings to take home. Never had she felt so at ease, so peaceful and safe. For one small moment her mind drifted to Stanley and the pain of his death threatened to swamp the pleasure of the day, and with no guilt for the first time, Elle pushed him to the back of her mind. She would release the thought another day but for today, just today, death had no place in her thoughts.

Keen to see more of the sloped-roofed building on the opposite bank, she took a gentle walk away from the scene. Her eyes sought out new wonders and her brain mentally logged new challenges. The small building sat neatly on the edge of the bank, and wild flowers dotted around the green fields either side. A sign offered the name of the property; Gibbonsgate Farm. Pulling her charcoal and paper out from her small valise, Elle settled onto a large wooden trunk lying sideways, and facing what she considered the prettier side of the building. Four small framed windows sat under a sloped roof, and not one could be classed as straight. Shadows, shapes and angles called out to her and soon the sounds of the mill pond, birds and rustling leaves on the breeze, were in the background of her mind, in the forefront; art.

'He sat just where you are now.' A woman's voice and the clanking of a tin pail interrupted Elle's flowing hand. 'N'owt but a lad when he first made a picture of this place. John the Scribblin' Artist, I called him, and Mary Lott the Mitherer was his name for me; before I married of course. I found a new man to mither when John took to travelling to paint.' The woman giggled. 'I didn't fuss or bother but simply ensured he was fed. Still he claimed I over-fussed. My brother enjoyed his company well enough. Willy, God rest his soul, would be most tickled to see a slip of a girl drawing just where his friend whiled away his time.'

Elle shaded her eyes to get a better view of the elderly woman stood before her. Clothing suggested she was not monied, in fact it suggested she was on the same rung of the financial ladder as Elle.

'You knew John Constable? The artist?' She enquired, knowing full well awe in her voice was evident. 'If that is the case, it is the second time I have sat and drawn where he did. Here, and Dovercourt Bay. How wonderful.'

'Knew him all my life. Loved him as one of my own kin. If you venture into the field, take care to shut the gate. Stay as long as you will but I have things to do. Fare ye well young maid.'

Before Elle could stand to shake hands and reply, the woman moved back to the house. Mesmerised by her movements, Elle grabbed another piece of paper and sketched out the back of the woman carrying her bucket. She wondered how many times Mary had been captured in much the same way by the artist she learnt more and more about each day.

'There you are!' The breathy tones from Angus hinted a touch of anxiety. 'I worried - but I need nay ha' bothered.'

Elle giggled. 'Your accent is strong when you tell me off. I am well, and I met a woman. She knew John Constable. Her brother worked the farm. Isn't it a delight of a place? The curves and points, the shadows under the eaves.' Elle's words tumbled out and Angus sat beside her. He reached out to her work and studied it carefully.

'My, you have captured the backside of the building well, and the pail adds to the eaves.' He teased.

'Oaf. That's the woman. I couldn't help myself. I just had to draw her - a memory of this place. Here, this is the farmhouse. If I recall she said her maiden name was Lott but the farm is

Gibbonsgate. Such an unusual name.' She passed him the drawing of the building. 'Where shall we head for now? I am starving. Should we eat here or would that be rude?'

'When you've stopped your chatter, I will get a word in. We will eat somewhere else. I have a place in mind. It will not disappoint, of that I am certain. I too managed a few sketches. A most interesting ripple of water drifted under the mill bridge. The light tripped down the centre and spread light branches giving the impression of lightening upon water. The image is clear and I have made notes. If we were anywhere else but here, I would be heading home for my studio.'

'Oh, Angus. I do understand. I am torn with wanting to surround myself with the glorious wonders of this place, and yet, I want to return to my palette and canvas. The week will give us both a project to keep us busy. Ready? Take me to the mysterious eating area.' She held out her hand and he pulled her to her feet.

'As I said. You will not be disappointed'. He strode off and his willing pupil followed.

Her gasps were audible when they moved from behind a thicket of small trees behind the other side of the building. Angus spread his arms outward, dropped his knapsack onto the floor, and waggled his fingers toward the scene in front of them.

'There you have it. No hay-makers or horse and cart but here it is, The Haywain, as Constable described so well with his brush.'

'It's breathtaking. Beautiful. The man is a wonder, I am most envious. When you showed me the printed picture of this place in your book, I never believed it to be real, and here I am, standing on the spot where a genius worked magic. What a perfect place to picnic, thank you, Angus. Thank you.' Elle swirled around to absorb the scene.

'I can see why he painted the farmhouse. The light falls in such a way that highlights its angles, and the shadows create new images in their own right'.

'It thrills my ears to hear you. My student listens and learns. Angus hitched his bag on his shoulder for better comfort, and place his hand on hers.

'Never stop learning. You have the makings of a fine artist. Your work will grace the walls of the keenest collectors in the country - nay- the world. Never give up your art, Elle. Never.'

Elle stopped walking, and with her arms outstretched and the ripple of a breeze teasing her hair loose around her face, she expressed her feelings in a breathless rush.

'Without it I cannot breathe. Angus, inside - deep inside - there is an ache, a raw pain of want. Art is all I have and all I can give, without it I am nothing.'

A silence fell between them as they walked back to the rail station. The dreaded beast sat snorting out smoke, surrounding passengers waiting to climb the steps for the return journey.

Tiredness may have taken hold on Elle's limbs but her mind, sharp, alert, and full of images, defied sleep. Angus wasted no time, his eyes remained closed the whole journey home. His head nodded forward and his chin rested upon his chest. Elle studied the man who, upon seeing her work, gave up precious time to encourage her dreams. A father figure. Elle resisted the urge to stroke his stubbled cheek in affection.

For me, he is my father and I will never let him down.

Upon her insistence he took one penny for sales of her work as commission, or for a lesson. Each time he refused but Elle needed to hold her head high and pay her way. He often told her to save her money for materials and travel. Find places to expand her mind; show the art world what Elle Buchanan could offer.

'If only I knew' she would say each time. The last time he responded to her words, she listened.

'You – the artist – need only create what you see. The observer will decide if it is for them. They will soon learn you offer quality visions; you just paint – let them make up their own minds.'

CHAPTER 18
Harsh Words Hurt

'If I was your mother I would have something to say about your living arrangements, but I am not therefore, I will hold my tongue'. Martha slurped loudly from her cup. Despite declaring she would keep silent, she bristled with an obvious need to speak her mind.

Elle sat running her finger around the rim of a china cup with a slight chip, and listened to Martha continue berating her for the unchaperoned trip to Flatford. Not once had it occurred to her that she had crossed any type of polite society boundaries. Given Angus was her friend and tutor why would anyone be so angry with her? Nor did she consider him a scoundrel taking advantage of a young girl, as Martha so loudly pointed out.

Elle's finger traced the rim of the pretty cup faster and faster, on the third turn her finger stopped at the chip, and she stared at it, then up at Martha.

'This is my life – this cup. Not a perfect circle but one with a blemish'.

'Stuff and nonsense.' Retorted Martha, and another loud slurp filled the room.

Elle opted for silence, and Martha's voice became nothing but a distant irritation echoing around the cottage. Shutting out the nagging tones, Elle, head down, allowed her own thoughts to air themselves inside her mind.

My mother should be in Martha's shoes, telling me the right and wrongs of the way I should conduct myself. My father; Angus's. Strangers care more for me than my parents. They are the chip and cannot fill the void. My friends care but I need to break free from restraint and restriction; to be me.

With sudden rush of clarity she understood what she wanted from life, and rose from the chair. Startled, Martha stood with her hands on her hips but Elle gave her no time to draw breath and re-launch her verbal attack.

'Martha, I understand your frustrations but forgive me when I say as much as you have offered the kindness of a mother, you are not mine,' she allowed the words to register for a brief second, 'a true sadness on my part as you make a fine Mama. With regard to Angus, he is my friend and I am his, nothing more. I do not benefit from the guidance of a loving mother with regard to men but your concerns can be quashed. I will heed your words, and thank you for caring.' Hoping the hurt she felt from Martha's words did not show, Elle gave a weak smile and sat down.

'Girl, I grow to love you, and can see why Rose and Stanley took to you. I worry about your future. That house. Why on this earth would Charles Gant be so keen to set it to rights? Forgive me but for no more than a chit of a girl bordering a beggar? What is in it for him I ask myself? Have you given any thought at all – of- of', Martha gave a discreet cough, 'how you are to repay him? Of what he expects from you? I pray he hasn't already received a payment. As for his son ...'

'Stop!' Elle's voice rose several octaves as she leapt to her feet. The pretty cup became dangerously close to having more than one chip and she steadied it with one hand. A hand she noted shook with rage.

'You think wrongly about Charles Gant. He merely honoured Stanley's wishes, nothing more. And before you wonder whether Stanley and I were lovers – no- no- *no*. He was my best friend; my brother. If you think I am repaying Mr. Gant with my body, then you do not really know me at all, nor I you. Forgive me but your words cut like a knife. I will take my leave as there will be words spoken that are best left in place, and I do not wish to live with regret. Your advice is unnecessary, I am neither weak nor gullible. Thank you for your concern – and tea. I wish you and Josh well, and will not return to visit. I thank you for any previous assistance but it appears my way of life offends, and I am not willing to alter my ways. It is the only life I have and I treasure each moment. Good day.'

Elle heard the chair fall to the ground but wasted no time in picking it up. Tears threatened but anger held them back. Martha had as good as called her a loose woman, and for that, Elle would never forgive. She held onto a secret and Martha would never learn the truth. In order to protect the secret and her pride, Elle knew she would need to leave the house, and the thought broke her heart.

She slammed the door of the cottage shut and ignored the calls of Martha for her to return. She strode with purpose from the yard and along the pathway to her home.

My home. Is it now a brand upon my brow? What have others been saying if those I thought cared for me could think such horrendous things of me? Do I carry a reputation that could harm Angus or even Charles Gant? What is to become of me?

Low clouds buffeted into each other as they made their way through a multi-grey coloured sky. Fierce winds blew wildly around her skirts and she lifted them from around her ankles. Puddles of muddy slime lay around, and Elle slowed her pace for fear of slipping. Much to her annoyance, the dull sound of a horse and cart rumbled behind her.

I am in no mood for Josh. I have no desire of arguing or pleading my innocence in a matter that is of no concern to either he or Martha.

She did not turn around, and the thuds could no longer be heard. Determined not to look back, Elle focused upon her home now in view. She loved the small cottage, and the thought of leaving sent shivers through her body. She pulled her cloak closer around her and stumbled onward, allowing tears of self-pity and sadness fall at will.

'You are cold, Miss. Buchanan.'

The chill of hearing Matthew Gant's voice so close to her ear brought forth a bout of nausea, and Elle lost her footing. She stumbled into a patch of muddy grassland, and cursed loudly;

with immediate regret. She gave him ammunition.

'My, my, you would make a fisherman blush dear lady.' Matthew's laugh and taunt angered Elle further. She scrambled aimlessly around in the mud, and only desperation and exhaustion made her take the hand he offered.

'We have an even status I see. Both have fallen in undignified fashion.' Matthew gave a mocking laugh, and Elle wrenched her hand free from his. She gave no thanks for his assistance and continued heading home fully aware he followed, and of her dirty appearance.

'Slow down madam. Do I not deserve a reward for assisting you?' His voice mocked and jeered but Elle kept her silence.

She reached the door to her home before she found courage to face him, and respond.

'Sir. My thanks for your assistance. As you can clearly see I am home and in need of tending to my clothing.' Elle shook her gown to emphasise her statement.

It irked her to see a sly grin form on Matthew's lips and of how attractive it made him look.

Turn away. Get inside. The man is a menace.

'If I were a gentleman I would offer my services. However, I am nothing more than a – what is it? Ah yes, a time-wasting scoundrel, that is should believe my mother's opinion of me. As I can see you are not injured – not physically, although if you are like me on that most unfortunate visit, you will have a bruised pride and ruffled ego. I will leave you to tend to your needs – reluctantly I might add, and take reassurance you are well. When I saw you making your way from the farmyard, you looked in a state of distress. Martha gave the appearance of anxiety and I feared you were unwell so followed. My apologies for startling you and causing you more distress.' He pointed to her face and Elle guessed the redness of eye from crying gave her away.

'Forgive me, Mr. Gant. It has been a day for unkind words and I am no company for a friend, let alone a mere acquaintance. I have no intention of offering bad manners but would ask you leave me in peace. I am due to visit your mother for another sitting in a few days, and no doubt our paths will cross then and I will be most respectful but today, I am dismissing you impolitely.'

She turned and entered her cottage. Matthew Gant walked away. This unnerved Elle, she expected him to put a foot in the door or make things difficult for her but instead he said nothing and merely walked back to his horse. She watched from the comfort of her warm home as he disappeared into the distance.

Damn you man. What game are you playing?

CHAPTER 19

Taking Stock

Sunshine poured in through the windows and Elle drew back the curtains to improve the lighting. Evangeline Gant sat with her usual withered look making the task of drawing a pleasant portrait somewhat of a challenge. The only time the woman spoke was to bark out orders to staff or to reprimand Elle for making her sit so long.

'I am a busy woman and sitting around so you can appease my husband is somewhat tiresome'. Elle doubted for one moment the woman disliked the idea of her portrait being centre of attention, and continued working without comment.

Barking dogs yapped excitedly outside the door and her subject glared at Elle.

'Time to finish. My husband has returned from his ride and I have no desire to see him in your company. Insulting.' Evangeline rose from the window seat and crossed the room. Elle ignored the snide remark. Her conscious was clear and she would not rise to the bait of goading and look guilty of a crime not committed.

'He has the audacity to bring you here under the pretext of painting but I am no fool.' The bitter words hung in the stale air of the room in a state of expectancy. Charles Gant's wife wanted a verbal war but Elle would give her no ammunition and continued packing away her tools.

'So, the little minx is silent. What, no declaring your innocence or his ...'

Her words were cut short with the door opening and both Charles and Matthew entering, along with two large Lurcher dogs who bounded their way to Elle. Charles Gant gave a nod to his wife but nothing more, and she stood, steely eyed, watching both men fill the room with their presence. Uttering only loud tuts to indicate her displeasure at the behaviour of the two hounds.

'Caesar! Trabor! Down!' Charles Gant's voice bellowed out his command, and Elle realising she held her breath let out a sigh when they slunk and lay down beside the large fireplace.

'Miss. Buchanan. Delighted to see you once again. How is the work coming along?'

Elle took his outstretched hand and shook it. She returned his smile, determined to show his wife there was nothing between them she replied in a steady tone.

'Mr. Gant. Pleasure is mine for I am in the good company of your wife and in your beautiful home. All is well and I am confident you will both be pleased with the end result.'

Matthew Gant gave an overdramatic cough and all turned to face him. To his credit, he blushed.

'Apologies. The very thought of Mama sitting patiently, and without complaint, is quite incredible. Forgive me Mother, but you are not the most patient of women nor, as you have frequently mentioned, not entirely happy with Miss. Buchanan being here for reasons unexplained yet obviously make you suspicious in nature.'

Elle watched as Charles swung a look to his wife, and son. He raised an eyebrow in question.

'Do I understand you have changed your mind about the portrait? Or am I to understand you have another reason to share your feelings with our son and not me. Suspicious. Of what pray? Speak woman.'

Elle's flesh tingled as the hairs stood on end upon her arms. Charles voice had a cold edge, and his wife paled. She no longer held an air of superiority but managed to outstare Elle, and share her cold nature with all in the room. She needed no words to convey her hatred of her husband and the girl she considered his mistress. However, Matthew had a look of triumph about him, and Elle guessed he enjoyed playing his parent's wits against each other. This was confirmed when he gave her the slightest of winks and grin. Elle, not wishing to be drawn into a family feud, turned back to her packing. A dog sighed and shuffled in its resting place, apart from that no one else moved. The Gant family reached a point of no return and Elle could not afford to be caught up in the aftermath. Somehow she needed to leave without creating any form of tension to the already volatile atmosphere. A slight sideways glance enabled her to gauge the clearest route to the door, and in one swift movement she collected up her goods and stood tall. She moved surefooted to the door and sensed all eyes upon her back. She turned and gave a fleeting smile, with what she hoped was a sincere sounding goodbye.

'Forgive me. I fear the light is fading, and I wish to make a start on the outline to canvas. I have no further need for you to sit for me, Mrs. Gant. I will contact when the painting is complete. Thank you for your patience. Mr. Gant. Mr. Gant. Good day.'

Matthew rushed to the doorway.

'Miss. Buchanan. We apologise. We have been rude and boorish with our family spat. I am certain I speak for my parents when I say please do not be a stranger to our home.'

A loud disapproving grunt came from the lady of the house, and Matthew shook his head in a manner of despair to show he disapproved of her behaviour. Charles held up his hands, and sent her another cold glare. A war had truly been declared.

'My son, for once in his life, has found his manners. I agree, rude and boorish. Forgive us, E – Miss. Buchanan. My wife has an overprotective nature and suspicious mind. Her twisted mind ...'

Anger welled and Elle could hold back no longer.

'Forgive me, Mr. Gant but your public disgracing of your wife belittles you, and I have no desire to stand here listening whilst you show her no respect. As for you Mrs. Gant, I suggest you clear your mind that your husband has any dealings with me other than with overseeing the wishes of a dead man. Mr. Gant junior, you should not interfere in the sorrow of your parent's marriage. You are spoilt and sly, and despite showing some sense of reason in the past few moments, have made me value my upbringing more and more. Poor and abandoned I may be but my parents instilled in me good grace and thought for others while they were in my life. Something you lack.'

Shrugging off the hand of Matthew, Elle shed the guilt of her secret. Charles Gant, a charcoal drawing and her payment were a thing of the past. A new found strength shimmied its way into her character and Elle knew it would never leave. All debts were paid and new pastures to be explored.

CHAPTER 20

Changed Characters

Bundles of outlined drawings and a part drawn canvas, sat alone in a trunk. Elle closed the lid and exhaled. The end of a painful experience and the start of a new road to travel lay ahead. For two weeks she cleared and sorted out her work. Angus sold many items on her behalf, and upon hearing her plans, forged ahead preparing the way forward for her.

A knock at the door startled Elle but excitement mounted. Angus was to visit today with information about her travel plans and her tickets. Pulling open the door disappointment and annoyance set in when she saw Charles Gant instead of her friend.

Appalled by his lack of respect for her privacy, an indignant Elle pulled herself to full height and found her sternest voice. In what she hoped was a firm, clipped message she wasted no time with polite society manners.

'Mr. Gant. I apologise, I have no time to spare you nor any conversation do I wish to have with you. All secrets of the past are just that, so do not worry yourself on that behalf. For your information, the house will be closed for a few months while I travel, and Mr. Argyle will care for my belongings. Unless you have anything of importance to say, I would appreciate it if you returned home or whatever hotel room it is you are inhabiting these days, and leave me alone. Good day, sir.'

Elle pushed the door closed but pulled it back swiftly when Charles Gant flung his arm in the way.

'Sir. I have no desire to do you physical harm and insist you leave my home immediately.' Elle's temper rose at his disrespect of her request for him to leave her alone.

'Miss. Buchanan. I heard of your intention to travel from your friend and came to wish you Godspeed. My apologies for arriving unannounced and after such a disastrous visit to my home. Sadly, my wife is stricken with a head pain and could not attend alongside me to offer her personal apologies, nor is my son available to join me. However, they have offered their apologies via my person. It is not my intention to cause you any distress in life. I fear you have suffered enough.'

Elle pulled the door open wider and stared at him in disbelief, then the laughter struck her and she bent double in amusement.

'Mr. Gant. If I thought for one moment your wife's apology was as genuine as her head pain, I would accept it, however, we both know she has offered no such thing so please do not treat me as a simpleton. As for your son, he did show a change in character when offering his apology on the day. Sadly, that day he became more of a man with manners than yourself, which does not put you in good light considering your son's normal behaviour. So, for the second time of asking, please leave. Your apology has been heard and accepted. I offer no thanks for it is my thought I deserve the apology. Please leave and never return. I may have been a bereft waif when you first knew me in that room in Colchester but I am now a woman in my own right and am no longer mouldable to the whims of others. This is my home by right of inheritance. You furnished it with our secret. I held my tongue and all is equal in that affair. Now leave, please.'

Charles looked down at her and his eyes lit up. He gave a wide grin.

'My dear young lady how true are your words. You have my upmost respect, you truly are a wise woman and no longer the frightened child. More of a lady than many I know. You have the ability to enter any level of class far higher than when we first met. I wish you well and say only this; should you ever need any assistance of any kind, please do not hesitate to contact me. I will always be available to you. Safe travels and I will enquire of you often through Angus as I am sure he will be informed of your safe arrival in France. Do keep him in the knowledge of your well-being as France is in a state of unrest, stay safe and again I say, should you need any support please ask.'

Elle nodded and gave a soft smile. No matter how angry he had made her, Charles Gant still found her worthy of supporting without forcing himself upon her. A gentleman born and bred.

'Thank you. We will part as friends for I wish never to have enemies in my life. Goodbye and I accept your kind offer. Should I find myself in need I will call upon you via Angus.'

She held out her hand and instead of shaking it, he leaned forward and kissed the back.

'For good luck.' He said.

Elle stood for a few seconds as he walked away before returning to packing away her bedroom belongings. Angus arranged with Josh to collect them when Elle left. She never made her peace with Martha, and Josh never interfered. Anytime their paths crossed they simply got along without any mention of what happened.

'My father and you have a secret if my ears do not deceive me.'

Matthew Gant's voice stabbed Elle as sharp as any knife. Her body froze. Slowly she turned.

'As I understand it sir, you overheard words and misinterpreted them. Pray, what are you doing inside my home, unannounced and uninvited? How long have you been here? How did you get in?' Elle's voice wavered, fear gripped her gullet and a faint threatened.

What does he want? What did he hear? She raced through the conversation between her and Charles, and realised with a sickness of heart that it could be interpreted in a way that did neither of them any favours.

'Firstly, I would like to thank you,' Matthew taunted, 'I showed changed character, and have more manners than dear Papa, in your eyes. Touching that he offered his support for your journey to Paris. After all, it sounds as if his money paved the way for many things for you after he knew you in

Colchester.' Matthew tut-tutted and waggled a finger at her.

'You have it all wrong.' Her voice came out in barely a whisper.

'Wrong you say? I think not. My father has a way of knowing women or should I say, young girls. You see, my mother turns a blind eye, and I, well I use my eyes, and now my ears have proved their usefulness. Wiley dog set you up nicely here.'

Elle straightened, and took a deep breath. It would not pay to goad him and she needed to rid herself of his presence without aggravation of any kind.

'Again I say, there is a misunderstanding. I became stranded in Colchester whilst looking for my parents, and your father offered a coin for food. Nothing was asked of me in return. To him I was a mere pauper child. Believe me, my bedraggled body would have interested no man. My being here is a coincidence of the greatest kind. I never knew him until Stanley died. It was Stanley who ensured the roof over my head. Please believe me. Your father and I have done nothing wrong – there is no secret other than the fact it is wise your mother does not have fuel added to a fire she burns.

Besides, I leave Harwich soon and there will be no point in continuing down a path that leads nowhere.'

Elle stared Matthew in the eye, she tried hard to convey some form of connection in the hope he would remain silent.

'You had a path laid out to follow? My father's that much is obvious. Love him, do you? Think the older man can offer more than someone such as myself? Mayhap you have only ever known the older man. If you wish to have taste of younger blood, I offer my services.' He gave a mocking bow and stepped closer. Elle smelled the alcohol on his breath and glanced over his shoulder to assess how far away from her main room entrance she stood, and what room she needed to skirt around him to safety.

With startling force, Matthew fell forward, and at the same time a resounding thud resonated around the room. Behind him stood Angus, a wide branch in one hand and his other outstretched to enable Elle to step over Matthew.

'What on earth did you hit him for, Angus? Is he dead? Please God do not say he is dead. Angus, check him. Why didn't you just call out?' Elle, frantic with panic, snatched the wood from her friend's hand and pushed him towards the body outstretched on her bed.

Angus shook his head and walked towards the man on the floor.

'A natural reaction. I thought he was hurting you. We met earlier and he could barely stand because of whiskey overindulgence. He boasted of his ability to take any woman he wished, and at any time. I pondered his words then realised he would attempt to get you alone. Word has it he is fond of taking advantage of young women.' Angus rolled Matthew over and looked at his face, then lifted his hand over the man's face. 'Still breathing; more's the pity. Fetch a bottle of whiskey, the one you keep for me. Are you packed?'

Elle raced to the bottle sitting on her sideboard, and handed it to Angus.

'I am, and ready to leave when Josh arrives. What will happen to Matthew? We can't leave him here.'

'He will only have a hazy recollection of this visit when I have finished with him. Working out reality from a drunken dream and bruises from a fall will keep him occupied for several days. You my dear friend will be long gone, and on your adventure. Paris is a lucky city, it will see you develop as an artist.

Study hard and you will reap the rewards from many of the best artists in the world. My time spent in France is one I will never forget nor regret. Gather your things together, go make peace with Martha while I deal with this one. This way Josh will not become involved, and his life made difficult at the farm. Your tickets madam, bon voyage, farewell, and write. Write often. Stay safe and trust only your sensible instincts for I am fully aware of how fanciful and impulsive you are inclined to be at times. Mr. and Mrs. Southgate will escort you to London. The Lordes, to Dover where Miss. McDonald will be waiting to escort you to France. The first part of your journey has been funded. My farewell gift. You know what to do when you meet Miss. McDonald. We are finished here. You must be away.'

Elle threw herself into Angus's arms, an action that surprised them both and she quickly stepped back. Neither concerned themselves with social etiquette when alone but Elle did not want to create an awkward situation before leaving her friend.

'I owe you so much. Thank you for arranging my chaperones. I promise to write often. I am weary with worry and excitement. You are certain all will be well with regard to ...' she pointed to Matthew.

Angus moved her gently away from his body.

'Unhand me woman. Be away with you and worry ye not about the fool. When he returns home his head will ache and whiskey will betray him. His visit here will become an addled dream, no more than that, and I wager he will not wish to find out whether you are home for a day or so.

Paris is waiting for you, leave all worries in England and enjoy a new adventure. Listen and learn from those who will readily offer their knowledge. Stay safe, and lead a sensible life. Return with new ideas. Embrace fresh ideas. Go. Time is of the essence.'

No need of any further reassurances, Elle gathered her valise and left her home. Angus encouraged her to take only the minimum baggage, and tempted her with the knowledge that sumptuous Parisian fashion awaited her coins, she refused, and purchased adequate clothes enough for her to carry. She did however, promise herself one gown of French silk when she arrived.

CHAPTER 21

Friendless Greetings

Celeste McDonald greeted Elle with a cold stare, and all new found courage left Elle within seconds of the withered glance. Determined to regain composure, Elle gave what she hoped was a sincere smile, and offered her hand in friendship. Sadly, her chaperone did not take up her offer but gave a sniff of disapproval in return. The hairs on Elle's neck tingled when the woman spoke. A harsh rasp of a voice with a hint of male deepness, and a stronger accent but not dissimilar to Angus's.

'The advertisement mentioned I would be escorting an English lady, not a quine who has seen better days.'

The growled words frustrated Elle, she could only just make them out through the thick Scottish accent. Not wanting the woman to gain the upper hand in the relationship with her dismissive attitude, Elle mentally dismissed the timid persona and drew herself full height with straightened back.

'Quine? I do not recognise the word but given the tone of your voice assume you insult me.' She barked back in the hope of extolling some authority. After all, the woman was employed by Elle to escort her to Paris, not the other way around.

'Nae. Young girl, you are nothing more than a country lass with no money. How d'yee plan to pay your way let alone my salary? Prove yourself, pay me.'

With impatient movements, and ones she hoped would get across to the woman that she was an irritation -a nuisance -Elle clipped open her valise. The vulgar act of publicly handing over money appeared not to worry the woman, who leaned in for a closer look. Memories of Evangeline Gant's manner with her staff, the straight back, pinched nose, and vocal firmness of being in charge, gave Elle the stance she opted to use against the battle-axed Scot. Forming her words in the most proper English she could muster, she handed the woman a small pouch.

'Here -half the purse of coins as promised. We do not have time, nor do I have the inclination to stand around on the quayside showing the world my savings. When you have earned the other half, I will give it to you. See? It is all there. Put the money away and we will board the vessel. It is apparent we will not be friends but I am ready to uphold the advertisement promise of employment. All I ask is you ensure I am protected against unwanted attention during our journey and to my destination. As for my appearance, you do not need to know my full story, simply accept I have employed you and can afford to do so. Shall we?'

Elle swept her arm outward to the gangway of the ship docked before them. Her stomach quivered awaiting a reaction from her travelling companion. The woman said nothing, her action as she snatched up her valise said it all. She was not to be trifled with but understood her position. She marched up the gangway and onto the deck. Elle took her time, she was in no hurry to spend more time than necessary with her disagreeable companion. Her one regret nagged away in the back of her mind; they were to share each other's company for a month while Elle found her feet. Once settled in Paris, Elle vowed she would ensure her sour-faced employee would be dismissed as soon as possible.

The crossing took its toll on both women as the packet steamer tossed around in the Strait of Dover. Elle tried to take in the scenery as they left port but it became obvious she was no sailor, and her legs failed her more than once. The nausea gave no sign of dissipating, and her hardy chaperone needed more support than she gave. Elle, frustrated with the fact she paid the woman to lie upon her bunk all day, ensured they were in each other's company for short periods only. Whenever there was a nausea-free moment, she stepped out on deck. Angus warned her about the advances of males and unscrupulous light-fingered passengers upon the journey, hence his hiring of Celeste McDonald, the now worthless chaperone. In honour of her friend's warning, Elle carried her belongings on one arm, and a stout umbrella upon the other. She kept her head down to refrain from eye contact with other passengers.

During these times she allowed herself the guilty thoughts of Matthew. Whenever she thought of him, yet again she could hear the imaginary voices of her elders berating her for such fancies. Elle simply could not shake him from her mind so opted to ignore the silent warnings.

'Bonjour, mademoiselle'. A male voice uttered words foreign to Elle, and she glanced up from her seat where she sat sketching pedestrians as they meandered past - anything to take her mind off of the dipping and rise of the boat – and Matthew.

Framing her eyes from the shimmering sunlight, she noted an extremely tall, whiskered man wearing the most outrageous attire she ever saw a man wear. Silk and lace trimmings made the outfit almost feminine in look, had it not been for the pantaloon styled trousers tucked into leather boots trimmed with gold braid. His hair, powdered white, sported a large blue ribbon at the point of a pony-tail. Elle suppressed a giggle. He looked overdressed upon their transport. His ill-fashioned outfit appeared to be made up of many centuries of style.

He held out an un-gloved hand, and sported a wide smile.

'Anglais?' Again he spoke in an accent Elle did not recognise but the rise and fall of sound he uttered appeared to be a question.

'Pardon me sir, I am afraid I do not understand. Forgive my manners but I am un-chaperoned and do not wish to dally with strangers.' She tried to express her best English using tones she overheard from the upper-class young women from her hometown. She closed her bag and rose from the seat, indicating her intent to leave his company.

'Forgive moi, mademoiselle. I have little English. My apology to disturb you. You drawings to me are good.'

'Sir, you have the advantage. I do not speak whatever language you use. I assume it is French? Thank you for the compliment with regard to my drawings. Now forgive me –moi? I must go attend to my friend below deck.'

The man bowed and his grin widened.

'You learn the Francais – French, non?'

It was Elle's turn to grin, and she gave a giggle. The badly attired man had a relaxed manner and she could not help but like him. He reminded her of a foppish, Angus. Just the thought of her friend dressed in the clothing in front of her created a bubble of giggles that burst through her lips before she could stop them.

'Oh dear. Non. I do not speak French. However, thanks to you sir, I can now say, me and no. Please, I really do need to leave.'

'I am arteest the same.' The man pointed to her bag. 'Jacques Devanté –

je m'apelle, Jacques. My name. You name?'

Elle laid down her bag upon the seat, and held out her hand. 'My name is, Elle Buchanan. I am flattered you consider me an artist. Where do you paint? England – France?' With something in common she was happier to spend more time in his company. If he was an artist as he claimed he may be able to guide her in some manner, as to where she would best seek out accommodation in Paris. 'I am heading for Paris once we disembark. I will need lodgings. My travelling companion and I will need somewhere to live while I study art in the city.'

The man sat on the bench and patted the seat beside him, Elle sat.

'I, how you say, journey to sell my work. Paris has my heart. We will travel to the city together. Your ami-friend he come too?'

Elle shook her head. 'My friend –ami is a woman. Scottish and my employee.' Seeing his confusion she explained slowly. 'I pay money. She help me stay safe.'

'I understand. So, where is this maid of yours? Why she not keep you safe?'

'She is not a sailor.' Elle made the actions of a boat rocking across water with her hand. The man laughed.

'So. When this woman is with you, you come to Paris with me. I have beaucoup d'amis, they sleep you.'

'Excuse ma manners fae leavin' you alane, Miss. Buchanan but I see you hae found someone ta amuse you. What I cannae fathom, is it from the theatre?' A loud Scottish voice boomed across the deck and Elle recognized the owner before even seeing her. She turned and glared at the woman who swayed and teetered her way across deck towards them. No-one could ignore the vapours of alcohol wafting from her being. She staggered into Elle with no apology and offered her opinion in a loud, slurred voice. 'I can see I came for air at the right time. You, take yoursel' away, insulting this young woman is nae way to conduct yoursel', I heard you offer to bed her.' Celeste McDonald stood full height, her accent much stronger than when they met. She stood by Jacques Devanté, and Elle compared the two. One was female and masculine, the other presented themselves the other way around. Celeste looked green about the gills and swayed from side to side whilst trying to berate the fancily dressed French man before her; the scene was farcical, and several passengers and crew thought the same. They had an audience but to Elle's embarrassment.

'Calm down, Miss. McDonald. I am quite safe. This gentleman was expressing himself in poor English. He is French –'

'Aye, I can see that. Fancy piece and more. Has friends who take advantage of young English women, I understood his words fear not, Miss. Buchanan. Yes, I understood them very well. Thay wee scunner.' She indelicately spat over the side of the boat, and Elle stood in shock at the woman. Her manners were virtually non-existent. Out of the two people in her company, she favoured the male as a companion. Even though he was the opposite sex, a foreigner and she had known him three hours less than her chaperone, she felt safer in his presence.

'Miss. McDonald. In view of the fact you have only seen and heard what you assume is happening, I think I should set you straight. Mr. Jacques Devanté is an artist. He saw me drawing and complimented my work, we talked in broken English and he has kindly offered us a lift to Paris. What he was explaining to me when you overheard, is the fact he has friends who can accommodate us, offer us lodgings. Unfortunately, his command of the English language only allows him to use words similar to those he wishes to express. I admire his ability to speak another language, no matter how poorly spoken.'

Her chaperone stared at her and muttered under her breath.

Jacques Devanté laughed. 'Words in your country have the same for me.'

Celeste glared at him. 'I dinna ken your meaning.'

Elle, aware that Jacques understood what Celeste muttered, interjected.

'I think it is quite safe to say he understood something you muttered. No doubt an insult. Sadly, I would not expect you to pay him a compliment. We are a mere stone's throw from France, and to be perfectly frank, you are proving yourself as an unsuitable chaperone. Your indifference and lack of respect, frustrate me.' Elle paused for a brief moment then before either companion could interject, she continued, her voice firm and controlled.

'Please consider your employment has come to an end. You have been paid half and earned virtually nothing, so I consider you paid in full.' She held up her hand to prevent the woman interrupting. 'There will be no discussion. We will part company at the quayside. You can purchase a return ticket with the money earned, it more than covers your costs. As I say, you have done nothing to earn the coins, and I prefer the company of those who have respect for others. I appreciate you felt I was in some form of trouble with this gentleman but on finding he is a new friend, you still insult him. In doing so, you insult my intelligence of being able to make new friends of good-standing. Please collect your belongings from the cabin, I will join you shortly, after I have informed the captain you no longer have access entitlement.' She held out her hand to the red-faced woman who tried to stammer out words but was over-ridden by the perfectly controlled, Elle. 'I wish I could say it's been a pleasure. Good day to you.'

Celeste McDonald stared in what Elle could only assume was astonishment, she turned to the French man spat indelicately at his feet, turned on her heel and walked away without a word. Elle looked at a bemused Jacques and smiled. She watched as the crowd dispersed.

'Mr. Devanté, your offer of a lift to Paris is graciously accepted. Thank you.'

Jacques fanned his face with a lace-trimmed sleeve.

'Mon Dieu. It was woman-oui?'

Elle laughed loudly into her gloved hand.

'Yes –er-wee –ooee, oh, yes, she is a woman.'

Secretly, Elle fancied that Celeste was wondering the same about him, and the thought bought about another burst of giggles.

'I apologise. I must seek out the captain and ensure that woman is kept out of my sight. Thank you again. I will return shortly.'

Jacques simply nodded.

Elle smiled. *What an amusing character the Frenchman is, I sense he is to be trusted far more than my Scottish companion. Paris cannot come soon enough!*

CHAPTER 22

Narrow Escape – A Letter Home

November 1st 1867
Rue Pigalle
Paris

Dear Angus,

I hope this letter finds you in good health. My journey is at an end, and I am settled these past three months. Forgive the brief message I supplied upon my arrival but you will understand my time has been occupied, and why, when you read this letter.

Sadly, the companion selected for the journey across the waters proved herself an untrustworthy character. It appears her legs were made weaker more by her drinking habit rather than the rough seas. She remained in our quarters, and failed to earn her salary. I dismissed her mid-journey. However, I am fortunate to have found a friend in a French gentleman of rather frivolous tastes when it comes to his attire but he is of good character. I feel I am quite safe in his care. He is in no way a threat to my person. This was recently proved when we were set upon by two men during our journey to Paris. They appeared to know exactly which valise to search for money – mine. Our lives were in danger from their inebriated knife-waving threats, and one wore the clothing of a sailor. They took everything I owned but walked away from Mr. Jacques Devanté's many trunks, in which he states were full of the finest cloth money can buy. It is suspected my travelling employee had something to do with the robbery, and was it is thought, to be a revenge attack.

Throughout the terrifying event, Mr. Devanté ensured my safe keeping, and has been active in finding me suitable accommodation. I have promised a full refund from the sale of my paintings. I sold my first painting of Paris to a friend of my landlady. Secretly, I think it is Mr. Devanté himself who purchased the work it was a street scene, and not a particularly wonderful piece. In your own words, "it could do with a little more attention to detail". Nevertheless, it was a step in the right direction.

Paris has captured my heart for its difference. My gracious, how different from the English the Parisian folk appear. The city is in a state of reconstruction so I am told, but people go about their business in a most relaxed manner.

The language is a barrier but I learn new words daily. I think you will agree my English is much improved, too. I study both in order to improve myself.

My friend, you were right to encourage me to come to France. Inspiration surrounds me. Although I miss your company, and lessons greatly, Mr Devanté has many friends in the art world, and they have embraced me into their groups.

Last month we ventured to the Exposition Universelle, at the Champ de Mars, a world fair of some proportion. It took my breath away. I could fill page upon page relating to the fascinating wonders we came across. Many a bronze sculpture captured my attention. Angus, it was truly magnifique – as Jacques declared many times over.

One particular friend, a Mr. Édouard Travet, is most encouraging. He introduced me to the neoclassic and Romantics. Work by Eugene Delacroix has become a favourite of mine, particularly his piece; Orphan Girl in the Cemetery. The angst captured in her face is mesmerising. Are you familiar with the painting – or indeed, the artist?

Édouard is well-known, and I have found a good teacher. Yesterday he bestowed upon me birthday gifts of canvas and oils. He claims I have talent, and in a few months he intends to hold a viewing of my work for others to enjoy. Imagine, my work on display in the centre of Paris, and other artists trying to understand what it is I try to portray on the canvas. I will share my friend, the very thought shakes me to my boots.

The evening light is upon us, and it is time for me to finish this letter to ensure its safe passage home to Harwich, via the man known as the facteure, (our postman). Please send news of home, and of the well-being of those known to me.

Again, please to not worry about me, Jacques can be trusted much as you can, Angus. We share the same pleasure of seeking out fabrics but he wears his silks in a far more elaborate manner. My two gowns are quite plain to his ruffled sleeved affairs. I fancy he has no interest in women, only art, for I have never seen him the company of a female aside from mine, and the friends of his friends.

I am now another year older and wonder what – and whom- it will bring into my life. This letter is written by a wiser woman than the one who left England, thanks to you, Angus. I was truly blessed the day Stanley introduced us.

*Stay safe and in good health,
Your good friend
Elle Buchanan*

***

Elle placed the envelope in the hands of the le Facteur, he was a neighbour and worked as a postman solely responsible for the delivery of letters to the necessary transporters abroad.

Always obliging, he ensure Elle received his full attention. Flattered, she tried not to encourage his flirtations as his bathing habits left a lot to be desired. Farm animals smelled sweeter, she remarked to Jacques on more than one occasion. With reluctance she needed to spend a moment in his company while he chatted about nothing she could understand. A polite nod here and there seemed to suffice, and he kept up his gushing flow. Eventually he noticed her shiver, and let her go. Elle made a mental note to purchase a warmer shawl for the winter evenings. Her new female friends offered clothing upon hearing about the robbery but not all items were suited to the inclement days ahead.

She watched the young postman walk away, and regretted not asking Angus to organise the shipment of the thick one she inherited from Rose.

Although happy in her own company, and that of her new friends, there were some days when Elle mourned those no longer in her life. The warm shawl would have given comfort at such times. Stanley, and his mother, would be proud of all she had achieved in Paris.

What of my own parents? Would they understand my need to paint? Do they think of me? Would I have made them proud, or thought it a waste of time? I will never know.

Before a melancholy mood could engulf her, Elle took herself back inside her small quarters; back to her painting. She worked on a personal piece, a memory canvas of those who entered her life, and those who were no longer beside her. It started out as a row of faces but became something far deeper, and drained her emotions whenever she turned the canvas to face the room. It held many a hidden meaning.

CHAPTER 23

Post From Home

Elle snatched eagerly at the letter in her neighbour's hand. His barrage of flirtatious winks, and what Elle could only assume was bribery for her to receive her letter, angered her. This was news from Angus, from home, and she had not time for an overgrown puppy-like male suggesting she planted kisses in return for something that was rightfully hers.

'Donne-le-moi!' She demanded in her most forceful voice. Possibly shocked by her use of French in such a tone, the man did just as she asked, and gave her the letter. Grateful to Jacques for her basic French lessons, Elle thanked the postman and rushed inside to read the contents of her precious letter.

***

Charles Gant Esq.
Gant's Farm,
Dovercourt,
England.

November 29th 1867

Miss Buchanan,

It is with regret I must inform you of the passing of your friend, and mine, Angus Eoin Argyle.

Cholera took several residents of the town, and Angus succumbed to the disease three weeks past, as did his housekeeper. He sent message to me that should I receive any news of you or your whereabouts in France, I was, (on his behalf), to thank you for your friendship, and to inform you to continue your artistic path. Continue to study hard, and he will watch over you. He had a fondness for you as he would a daughter.

His affairs have been attended to as per instruction, and his body is buried locally. I personally ensured he had a decent burial, and not a communal one. Upon your return to England, I will show you his resting place. Fortunately, I have friends in places, and am owed a wager or two.

I took the liberty of opening his correspondence, and to my good fortune I found your address.

Angus left all legal affairs in good order, and is in the hands of my solicitor, I am the executor of the will. Angus entrusted me with his wishes, and all he owned has been placed in your name. He has no other family, and as he said, you were as a daughter to him. I am to become the guardian of your affairs. With this in mind, and reading of your robbery, I have arranged for you a small fund to repay the gentleman, Jacques Devanté, and enough for you to purchase new attire. Each month I will issue sufficient funds for your comfort. The first of the money will arrive within a few days.

It pains me to be the bearer of bad news via the pen, as I know how much our mutual friend meant to you. We enjoyed the company of an upstanding, creative, talented gentleman.

I do pray you have a friend by you to comfort you in your time of need.

Should you wish to return to your home please write, and I will ensure it is ready for your arrival. I have taken the liberty of asking Martha to keep it clean, and aired. Angus had the key sent to me upon realising the seriousness of his condition, and news of his housekeeper's death. It is my understanding she was originally in charge of its upkeep.

Miss Buchanan, we parted on difficult terms but is my wish we start afresh.

You asked Angus to send news from home. Not much has happened since you set off for pastures new. The port is busy, and there are signs of development of the town, however, beyond that I have nothing more to add.

My personal news is my son is recovered from a misfortunate accident. He took stock of his situation, and is, I am happy to say, a reformed character. A son to be proud of, and whose company I enjoy.

My wife? Of her there is little change, although today she has complained of a fever. I must say I saw no evidence of a fever when she berated the dogs for dragging the carcass of a rabbit into the house. Her portrait hangs in pride of place, and I think of you each time I pass it by, you do have an extraordinary talent. A grand likeness. Thank you for instructing Angus with its installation.

Again, my sincere apologies for the news in this letter, and my condolences for the loss of your friend.

Please send note when you have received your funds, to rest my mind you are taken care of financially.

Regards
Charles Gant esq.

CHAPTER 24

Missing Desire

Each stroke of the brush held an emotion, Elle's movements became a frantic dance of colour collisions and blending. Time and time again she stepped back to critique her work, and her heart poured onto the canvas until the daylight switched off her mind.

Evening gave poor light but her task was complete, and tiredness weighted her shoulders to a slump. Her small bed invited her to rest awhile, and Elle heeded its call. She curled into a foetal position and allowed her body to relax. Within moments her mind relented, and Elle slipped into a world of calm and satisfaction. Her first true piece of art instilled in her a sense of completion. It had been a week since the news of Angus's death set her upon a heart wrenching journey.

Hustle and bustle noises from the streets below disturbed her slumber and the high-pitched voices from the café across the road informed her dawn had moved into mid-morning. Coffee mingled with fresh bread aroma drifted through the garret window and overpowered the stench of the street for the first time since she arrived. It was as if her senses had found a new level, and any that were not acceptable were simply overridden by the more pleasant ones. The same appeared to be happening with the noises below. A new appreciation of her surroundings came upon her, and Elle remained still, absorbing the atmosphere. She sensed the birth of a new memory, and something had changed.

Oil paint fumes added a touch of seduction, a tingling of the senses. Her love of her surroundings, along with her passion of the raw beauty of Paris ached inside her belly. Angus's death pained her as much as Stanley's had, yet the joy of releasing the true artist within gave Elle peace to accept the gift he gave her in life. His vision of her future, his faith in her ability, his love for her as a friend – daughter.

A dull thud against her door brought her back to reality. Her tranquil moment, disturbed. Exhaling an irritated sigh, Elle clambered from her bed, and brushed down her gown with stained hands.

Next time remember to undress. You are a crumpled mess, Miss. Buchanan.

'Oui. Who is it?' She called out while crossing to the large panelled door.

'Jacques. Jacques Devanté. Veuillez ouvrir'.

Recognising both voice and meaning, she opened the door but not before running her fingers through her hair. She knew Jacques would chide her for looking slovenly. He always dressed with impeccable precision. She often teased him for being more feminine in his desire to impress others than she. He always retorted with the fact she was English and had no sense of style, nor had she any pride in her appearance. Their friendship grew upon the delicate insults they threw at one another during their verbal teasing.

'Bonjour'. Jacques face said more than words could express. He tutted and muttered in French but Elle knew he was commenting upon her appearance.

'If you are asking how I am, I am well enough, thank you. Saddened by my news from England but work allowed me to express my sadness, hence my dishevelled appearance that offends your vision so greatly.' Elle smiled at her friend, and took the bread and wine he proffered.

He walked to the canvas turned towards the wall.

'You 'ave been busy painting into the night, yes?'

Elle broke off a piece of bread and bit into it, starving to death was not an option and she realised she had not eaten for over a day.

'Oui. I found a topic which released my inhibitions. A fever came upon me and I simply had to paint. It is complete. I have no need, nor do I wish to alter any one thing.

Jacques clapped his hands in child-like delight.

'Magnifique! Please?' He pointed and lifted the canvas still on its easel so it faced into the room.

Elle held her breath. In the painting she captured exactly what she wished, and inwardly hoped others would interpret it as she intended. Would she still see her creation in the stark daylight - would her vision look back at her as it did several hours previous?

Crimsons, black, a variety of golden shades, and sea-green colours of home filled the room. The light caught shadows and enhanced their depths. Rays of sunshine bounced from colour to colour inflaming each section with the need to be viewed. Familiar faces looked out from hedge-rows, flower beds, the river Seine, and each face looked upward to the top of the Arc de Triomphe, and St. Nicholas Church from home, her monuments of representation, and the centre of focus. Within the walls were several images of Elle in varied states of expressive emotion. Her subjects all looked to Elle with their own expressions embedded deep within their eyes, and she back at them.

It was a masterpiece. Each face came with her from England to remind her of how strong she could be in the face of diversity. Each one a memory of a life lived, and to be lived.

She looked to Jacques, he stood with his hands on his hips, his slight figure rocking back on its heels, his brow creased and his tongue rested on his teeth, he appeared deep in thought. Elle sat down on the edge of the bed and held her hands to her chin as if in prayer. She watched him drink in her work. Silence surrounded them, and Elle, confident her piece was as perfect as she hoped, willed him to envisage the same.

Tears dropped onto her lap, startled, and completely unaware she cried, Elle looked back at her painting through blurred eyes. Her life looked back at her. Monuments of Harwich and Paris, along with her soul, blended together in shades of torment, wonder, fear, love and serenity.

Jacques broke the silence with a dramatic sigh that filled the room. He flexed his hands and rolled his shoulders. He flicked his head side to side as if reading her work, muttering words Elle could not understand.

'Jacques. English. Please.'

'Ma Colombe. My Dove. You 'ave captured your life, oui? So many emotions. I see pain, love and angry - anger. But forgive me, I have troubles. The English heart in you still has the lock with the key - I see no, loving, no lust. No love of a woman, only the love of a girl. Ne pas?' He stomped his way around the room, and then went back to the painting.

'Why you not share the desire for him? His eyes hold a secret you are unwilling to share. You hold back on your want for this man. The work is tres bon. Spectacular, stupéfiant - breathtaking but you - how you say - lack in – non -you have forgotten, *desire*.'

Elle, shocked by his words, rose from her seat. She walked over and looked at the male Jacques pointed to - never had she considered any part of her would have desired him in the manner Jacques suggested. She shook her head.

'You read his eyes in poor light, Jacques. Mayhap, confusion but not desire. The painting exhausts me. When it is dry I will wrap it and store it away. It will never see daylight again. I considered it for showing but now I am not so sure. I do not think people will understand the meaning behind the painting. They will want names for the faces, and I cannot share them, they will want me to label the painting, and I cannot. Now I am not so confident.'

Jacques pulled out a chair from under the small table by the window. He poured himself wine from the jug, and as Elle had, took a moment to stare at the activity in the street below.

'You have scared. No?'

His question drew a giggle from Elle, and she responded with a light-hearted retort.

'No, Jacques. I do not have scared. I have subjects who play with my heart. People who have hurt me in some way. I am not scared of sharing the painting, I am just not sure I wish to confuse people with it, or answer questions I do not understand myself. You saw something missing; I do not. What would others see?'

Jacques walked over to her, he lifted his hand to his heart, and stared intently into her eyes.

'They would see the same as me – a young woman in love but have the fear to exprimer – show the love - desire.' He poured more wine, and topped up the glass in Elle's hand. 'You need the relax. Life to live. How you say …'

Elle interrupted his passionate flow. Some days she found his intense conversations, tiring.

'I live life, Jacques. My life is rich with art, and I am not in love. You are mistaken. There is no man in my life. Even less now I have lost my friend Angus. Yes, that one.' She nodded as Jacques pointed out the red-haired Scotsman in the painting.

'He was more my father, and most definitely not a lover. That man is the reason I am here, he was my tutor. This one, my true father, and he, he has no love from me.'

Jacques knew her story, and gave slow shake of his head, he understood. He pointed out Evangaline. 'I pray she is not Mama. Eyes of a snake. This one, he is inside your heart, and has your love. You paint it well – it is the frere – brother, yes?'

Elle shook her head. 'No, he is not my brother, and yes, he is inside my heart. He is Stanley, the truest friend I will ever know. Remember how I told you he came to my assistance. This one, she is his mama. I loved, love them both. Snake Eyes is the wife of this man. He is now my guardian. He once gave me a coin but he is a friend of some distance.'

Jacques gave a loud dramatic sigh, placed his hands on his hips and stared at her hard. He turned sideways to the painting, and once again pointed his slender finger.

'Still you do not share me this one.' He pointed to Matthew. 'This one is inside your heart. It is closed to him but he is there.' He pounded his chest to indicate the heart. 'There is no light in his eyes, you hide in … you should paint the light of love but you cannot. Your brush, it tells truth story. Truth story the world should see. That is what we want to see, love lights. Paint again, paint the light into his eyes. You penser – think you have hidden love but the world will still see it within the nothing. You speak loudly by giving him no love lights.'

Elle, frustrated by his insistence that she loved Matthew, chose not to respond. She raised her glass, and with the boldness of someone intoxicated but not yet fully drunk, she jumped to her feet, crossed over to the painting, raised her glass, and at the top of her voice, she declared. 'To Angus. My friend. Rest in peace.' She burst into tears and allowed the tears to flow free.

'Repose en paix. Rest in the peace. To friends and love, Elle. Friends and love.' Jacques laid down his glass and in one swift movement, Elle snatched it up and downed the contents in one gulp. She rushed to the decanter on the dresser across the room, and poured another. She turned to salute the painting, and again drank the wine at such speed, Jacques could not stop her.

She stumbled toward the decanter for another draft but this time he managed to move it from her grasp. She swayed and he held her in his arms. Murmuring soft-toned words she did not understand, he manoeuvred her to the bed, and she laid down. Jacques kissed the back of her hand.

'Sleep. You must rest. Forgive me for the upsetting. I will return le matin.'

Elle said nothing, she allowed the warmth of the wine wash over her. It blocked out the memories that threatened her self-preservation. She could not afford to let the past haunt her, the present swamp her nor the future scare her. She needed to block out the truth of her emotions.

Jacques reached the door when a loud knock startled them both. He pulled open the heavy oak door to be greeted by a face he had seen not a few seconds gone. He turned to Elle. She stood upright and started towards the visitor but her legs buckled from under her, and for the second time in her life she fainted.

CHAPTER 25

The Awakening

Elle ran her tongue around her mouth, the dry sour sensation made her gag. She struggled to rise from her resting place, and when she did so a pounding beat inside her head warned her to stay where she was comfortable. She shifted her position, and pulled the coverlet back over her shoulders.

Hushed voices across the room became louder, and she could no longer ignore the fact she was not alone. The door closed with no regard for her pulsating headache. One of the voices left the room.

'Jacques?' Her voice sounded as weak as she felt.

A cold cloth soothed her forehead.

'The wine disagreed with you.' A familiar male voice told Elle what she already worked out for herself but hoped it was just a dream.

'Jacques?' She repeated, but although she knew the answer, she could not comprehend the situation.

'I think we both know I am not your French lover. He has gone in search of accommodation for me. I tried to explain I would not require rooms but he is quite a determined man – assuming that is indeed what he is – a man.' The familiar mocking tones of Matthew Gant's voice were too much for Elle, and brushing aside the self-inflicted frailty, she pulled herself to full height.

'What in Heaven's name are *you* doing here? How dare you arrive unannounced and then proceed to insult my friend – please note I said friend. Your crude assumptions are too much, you rude boar – and yes, I mean the animal, of a man! Get out of my home. Leave!' Elle clutched onto the counterpane with such force her knuckles ached. How her hands itched to slap the face of the unexpected, unannounced visitor before her. Matthew was in Paris and it unnerved her to the core.

What does he want? Revenge? Her mind raced with reasons as to why he stood in her room, arriving unannounced.

Matthew made a snort sound. 'Calm down, Miss Buchanan. This wild boar is not here to seek revenge for our last encounter. Oh yes, I remember it with great clarity. And so you might blush. I suffered immensely thanks to the heavy hand of your now dead friend. Fear not I am here at the request of my father, I carry money for your upkeep. It appears you are a fortunate young woman; Angus Argyle left you in a comfortable position. With my father's attention, the home he set up for you, and now the inheritance of your *friend*, one can honestly say the men in your life have treated you well. Mayhap you groomed them well enough and now reap the reward. Is that the case with the French fancy who appears to *know* you well enough that you entertain him in your *boudoir?*'

The slap resounded around the room. Elle no longer held back, and Matthew felt the full force of her hand.

She said nothing, her actions relayed her message, and her arm trembled as she held it towards the door.

Matthew threw down a leather pouch, and grinned back at her.

'Your payment. Good day. I will wait outside for your *man* to return with the address of my residence. I bid you farewell, and do hope you are in better spirits when we meet again.'

'Get out!' Elle threw the purse in his direction. His words hurt her more than she would ever allow him to know. The purse caught the edge of the cloth covering her latest creation, and it slid to the floor. Elle glared in horror at its crumpled traitor-like state. The painting presented itself in all its glory, and Matthew glanced sideways then turned to gain a better view. His face no longer held a mocking grin as he looked upon face upon face. Faces he knew well. He moved his hand upward towards the image of Elle but before he could touch the canvas his arm was pulled away with force.

'Don't you dare lay your hands upon my work. I asked you to leave, now go.'

Elle, struggling with anger and nausea, held onto his arm in defence of her painting – and dignity.

'Elle.' His voice soft and as if in awe, whispered her name. 'It is truly a work of art. The eyes are like windows, one can see into the soul of each one. You humble me with your ability to capture feelings and portray them in such away; it is much like a mirror. I feared you captured all I feel for you in my eyes but it saddens me to see only blank, black spaces. If only, in real life, you would look at me the way you do in this painting, and look into my eyes to see the me inside. I wonder then what my eyes would hold. I wonder what you hope to see in return. I would like to think the vision of you looking at me is of a woman looking to the man she desires. Sadly, I am convinced this portrays opposites and positives, the opposite for me would be as you look at me now, live, in the room. Hatred and disgust. If only it were the face of the girl – woman, on the canvas.' Matthew gave a loud sigh of resignation, and shrugged off her arm.

'You win madam, I will leave. I have said things I will always regret. I came to capture your heart but now know there is no heart to capture, purely a void filled with the faces who haunt you. You need no words to explain your feelings or to express your truth. You need only a paintbrush. It is as damming to me as a pistol through the heart. You painted through your eyes – if only I could turn back time.' Matthew lowered his head as if in sorrow.

Not certain of whether she should ease his pain of disappointment by explaining he read the portrait in the wrong manner, and that she dare not show what she wanted to see in his eyes, Elle remained silent. She walked to the water jug, she needed to quench her thirst.

Aware of her sour breath she sipped the remains of a lavender and violet cordial. Her throat tightened against the perfumed water but she swallowed and sipped as quickly as she could. Her thirst satisfied, and the heaviness upon her tongue diminished she ran her fingers through her hair, straightened it into a tidy knot and tied it with the ribbon draped over the back of the chair. The sight made her smile, Jacques and his finicky ways – her French Stanley, a caring man.

She played for time, not daring to speak, and fully aware Matthew was still in the room.

Go. Leave. Let me in peace.

Her actions were slow and steady, and she avoided any eye contact. It was obvious he had no intention to leave despite his threats to do so, his arrogant air had left him and Elle watched from the corner of her eye as he turned back to the painting and studied it with deep intent. He searched the painting, and Elle could only assume he still sought for something positive in relation to them both. She knew only black eye sockets would stare back at him, that his search was in vain. Elle found a barrier when it came to her feelings for Matthew, they were different to those she had for others in her life. Until this moment she saw only dark desire whenever he looked at her, should she take up a paint brush that instant, she would be able to paint a different Matthew, a softer soul. The though frightened her, to do so would mean letting down the barrier that protected her heart, something she would never allow another to break. She made a solid vow after Angus died, no living being would ever be allowed to bring her to her knees when they left her alone in the world. She could no longer afford to give of herself, it would destroy her.

'You claim to try and capture my heart. If that is so, why do you strut around with such pomposity and arrogance? Sir, I fear you shrivel my heart with your acid tongue and cynical manner. You treat me as a woman of the Latin Quarter, a woman of the night. Each moment I am in your company you attempt to belittle me, to unnerve me and in the past, made me uncomfortable in your presence. Capture my heart?' She gave a half-hearted laugh, and again pointed to the door. 'I think we both are aware this conversation is at an end. Good day.'

Matthew gave a slight inclination of his head, he reached out and gathered his hat and gloves.

His face, full of a sadness Elle never dreamed she would see, paled.

'My sincere apologies Miss. Buchanan. I mishandled the situation. Please give my regards to your friend, and inform him I am to return to England on the next available packet. Our paths will never cross again, I am fully aware of your feelings toward me, and wished I knew of some way to remove the past hour, and be allowed to show mine to their fullest. I will inform my father of your wellbeing and bother you no more.'

Elle held her breath until the door closed, she listened for the familiar click of the lock falling into place, and rushed to the window. She waited until his footsteps finished echoing on the stairwell, leaned over the window ledge as fare as she dare, and watched his round-shouldered figure walk away. The walk of a defeated man. His broad shoulders no longer upright and proud, and his walk no longer the long stride, thigh-bulging swagger she enjoyed from the rear in the past. Realisation took seconds to reach Elle's confused mind.

He loves me. He truly loves me.

CHAPTER 26

Feaux de L'amour - Love Lights

Many people nodded and smiled, and Elle simply gave a gentle nod of polite, friendly acknowledgement. It had been a long day and her jaw ached from smiling, and her hands were tender from so much enthusiastic handshaking. The double cheek-kissing embraces still amused and confused her English upbringing, so she tended to shake a hand and take a step backward before her face endured another customary greeting.

Her painting, now proudly displayed by Travet as an added guest display within his own, had been christened by Jacques. *Feaux de L'amour*, attracted many positive exclamations. Elle enjoyed seeing people chatting in small groups and pointing to her work but it was not all pleasurable.

From a distance Elle could see the dark eyes of Matthew stare accusingly across the room. How she wished she could paint the true love lights she yearned to express. He had not visited her again, nor had he sent world in any form, and she accepted he had returned to Harwich. Over the past three weeks she had written note after note but burned each one. Jacques offered to go fetch him from England but she brazened out the reason for her miserable state as simply the fact her parents' faces gave her a melancholy air. Whether he believed her or not, Jacques never said.

A few days later he bought Travet to speak with her.

'You are ready to show the world your work. It is time, do not argue. Show me something to share with Paris.' The artist spent no time in ordering her to bring him work. Elle showed him autumnal scenes from Montmartre, river scenes from the Seine, and floral displays in various forms.

'Zut alores! You insult me child. Show me something with substance, with the passion. You English with your reserved straight shoulders – give me what you 'ave learned in France!' Travet turned to Jacques and belched out what Elle could only assume were a string of insults. Her friend stomped over to the far side of the room, his heels clattered upon the boards. His temper was up, and Elle sensed a rage between the men. She had seen artists flare up at each other when she strolled the embankments. The French had a theatrical temperament when it came to a misunderstanding. Travet had disturbed Jacques into action by his words, and they appeared to be words that angered. With a steely stare he looked to Elle for assistance with lifting out the canvas that leaned against the wall. She shook her head. He grunted back and stomped his foot in a child-like tantrum.

She turned to Travet. 'Sir, it is not worthy of display. It is merely the attempts of a girl in distress; me. I tried to portray a passion I know nothing about. Jacques, for a reason known only to him, has fallen in love with the piece but it is incomplete. He calls it, *Love Lights*. I see only darkness. This sir, is my life – or rather the images of those who have touched it since my birth. I have had only a few enter my life but the majority have left … '

'Silence. I do not have the time for the family 'istory. Art. Show me art. Not pictures of tree-lined streets with cold-limbed imbeciles holding paintbrushes on every corner. I demand art. I was *promised* art!'

The man's face was as claret as the wine Elle poured into his glass. She desperately tried to pacify him before he exploded across the room, such was his agitation.

'My friend flatters me if he considers my work art, and worthy of showing you, sir. You have permission to look into my mind but should you leave lacking insight into what I am attempting to convey, please do not say were not warned. Jacques, remove the cover please.' Elle enacted the unveiling and watched Jacques lift the cloth as if removing clothing from a baby, with gentle tenderness. Elle smiled as he stepped back from the easel and bowed quite an unnecessary floor sweeping gesture. Travet, soothed by the wine, took great steps to shoo his friend away. He drained his glass, gestured for another, and took his first glimpse at the painting. No sound dared reveal itself in the room; the atmosphere taut with anticipation.

Travet looked closely, he stepped backwards, took another close look, and stepped backward again. He lifted a candle to improve the light, and shadows skipped across the canvas. He sighed, placed the candle back onto the dresser and clicked his fingers at Jacques, and nodded toward the window.

He slurped at his wine with no heed for manners, while Elle scuttled around making room for Jacques to place the easel and canvas in position. The remains of the sunlight teased its way into the room as he pulled back the drapes. No words were spoken in the cramped room, and Elle longed for air, to run away and break free from the tension.

It is only a painting, Elle. Calm down. What is the worst that could possibly happen? He doesn't like it – it is not the world's end. It is just a painting.

A snagged nail captured her attention as she talked to herself in silent conversation. A few seconds later a loose thread on her gown entertained her.

Say something man. Speak. Leave. Just stop torturing me!

She concentrated upon so many small things in the room that when Travet finally spoke it made her jump. His words were in a smattering of French and English. They gushed from his wine-stained lips.

'Magnifique! Captivating. Véritable art! True art. Miss Buchanan, this is the painting I seek. This is the one I will display. Burn all others, you do not need to be trapped by mind-suppressing gutter contents. There is fire in the belly. There is beaucoup de passion dans Feux de L'amour. Much passion. Ah, the eyes of love, the love lights. Magnifique!'

Elle had quite forgotten Jacques was in the room as she watched Travet gesticulate and ramble out his compliments in wild abandon, that when Jacques shrieked with delight she lost balance and supported herself against the back of a chair. She could see his hands moving in clapping motion, and watched his lips move, not understanding the words he expressed. Watching two Frenchmen celebrate was exhausting.

She whispered out the name. 'Feaux de l'amour. A most romantic sound. A loft title for an ill-painted piece but a grand name nonetheless. My lines are not yet professional, my strokes a a haphazard mix of lessons learned and a need to express. Surely you cannot be serious in wanting to display this amongst your masterpieces, Monsieur Travet?'

Her guest twisted his body into a more comfortable position and faced her. Elle noted the crease created by a frown upon his brow. He clicked his tongue between his teeth, and stared her down. His voice remained with her long after he left the room.

'It is a masterpiece my child. Painted by a true artist. An artist yet to find true love, the love that lasts a lifetime. The black eyes speak louder than any words. The black eyes fill me with dread, for when you paint their true colour, I fear you will have no love left for Paris remaining in your heart, she will lose you, be replaced by the love. Paris has only just found you, she wants to love you. Do not leave her before she shares you with lovers who need to see the dark eyes before they find the flame of love – before you find you have suppressed love.'

He grasped her hands, and his voice held such emotion Elle fought back the urge to cry. 'We cannot lose you but you have to let love guide your work.'

Travet muttered words in French to Jacques, and Elle stared at her picture, stunned by his words.

Do not leave her before she shares you with lovers who need to see the dark eyes before they find the flames of love. Such powerful words. I have seen Matthew's dark eyes, now I need to find the flames of love and relight them. I must return to England.

CHAPTER 27

Sacrifice

Jacques voice rang around the room. The sound reverberated tinny tones from the pans he stood beside. Elle winced as the hollow sounds tingled within her ears.

'Explain me. Understand to me! You behave …' he raised his leg and stomped his foot for dramatic emphasis in an attempt to explain himself.

His opinion of her was one of an ungrateful child. A child who did not realise the opportunity before her. Travet was a man with talent and fame, she would not meet another like him, and you do not insult such a man in the manner she intended.

'Why you run to England? A cold land of closed hearts … pourquoi? He slammed his hand onto the table. 'Why you think love waits for you within the heart of the imbecile brute?'

Elle's temper flared. For an hour she allowed her friend the opportunity to express his reasons for her to stay but now he overstepped the boundary of friend to dictator.

'It was not so long ago you were prepared to drag him back to me – for me. We are friends, you and I. The decision for me to return to my homeland is mine. Grateful as I am for all you have done for me, I have the right to make up my own mind. Yes, I am fully aware of what opportunities I am to leave behind but my heart is no longer in Paris. I am choked with a black mind – I see nothing – nothing. I fear if I stay I will have painted the last image from my mind. I will be modelled into someone else; a fancy artist of Travet's creation. I need to see the shores of Dovercourt, the fields of Flatford, the hillocks of Ramsey.

My passion, my heart, my life – it is all there – I live there and feel alive, I exist and learn here. There is a difference, a vast difference. I cannot walk alone here. I cannot clamber the rocks, your rivers smell but not as beautiful as the marshland of home on a winter's day – damp soil not damp sewerage. The wind blows here but it does not clear the melancholy of a lost soul. I need to walk the coastline, to shout at the waves, to …'

Jacques banged his hand on the table for a second time.

'And you –penser – think your man will be there, waiting, non? A rogue of a man who will strip you of your art. You need to rester – stay here with me. Grow in Paris – mourir – die in England. Words they leave me. I have the angry with you.'

Elle opened the door head down, tears dripped onto the wooden floor and she watched as they spread and stained where they dropped. Silence fell between her and her friend. She could no longer cope with his rant or anger, it was so very different to his usual dramatic tantrums.

Jacques gathered his things. 'Vous êtes fou.'

Elle sniffed back the tears, wiped her face with the cuff of her blouse, and looked at the man whose words tore at her insides.

'Leave. I am not crazy. You hurt me with your words, Jacques. If I die in England I will die happy, and at home. Paris has allowed me to learn who I am, and what I want from life. For that I am grateful. Our conversation is turning sour, and it is best you leave.'

Jacques walked over to her, and she folded her arms. The action gave her strength and courage against what she feared might be an embrace.

Jacques tilted her face to his. 'Cry. Then make to you the understanding of painting in France is best for you. My words end; I have no more.'

Elle removed his hand from under her chin, she held open the door.

'I have two to share. Sans regret – no regrets.'

Slowly she closed the door, and listened for him to walk away but he remained still. His footsteps took a moment to tell her he had left the building and crossed the courtyard. She remained leaning against the closed door. Sadness swamped her but if Jacques were to return the next day her mind-set would remain the same; determined to return home.

Time dragged on and she paced the floor. Decisions needed to be made, her dream-chasing days were over. She sat by the window and pushed it open, poured a glass of wine, made a silent toast of thanks to Paris, and allowed her mind to drift into memories of her time spent amongst the people of the city. Not one of them had been unkind, and she refused to face the fact she had probably lost another close friend. The pain of realisation was too much to comprehend, too much to bear.

She spent many of the night hours in turmoil, and laid awake in the darkness and deliberated over the sacrifices she would be making with her return home.

CHAPTER 28

Into The Bosom

Dampness cloaked Elle, and foggy patches and ghostly rolling mists surrounded the marshlands but never had she felt so alive.

The mud-paved pathway to her home shared its loneliness. Endless rows of overgrown grasses and evergreen hedges showed only limited visitors had ventured to the small cottage leaving sporadic hints of neglect.

Despite having offers of transport to her door, Elle wanted to take the walk home along the path. She wanted to breathe in the air, and gain a sense of belonging once again.

'Home. It *is* where my heart lives.' Elle declared to no one but herself. She stomped down thistles as she strode along with purpose. Evidence of roses past their bloom glistened with dewy cobwebs, and Elle made a mental note to cut them back the next day. Smoke spiralled upward from the chimneystack, it clung to the slow drifting fog and Elle mused as it painted images in the sky.

I'm grateful Josh received my message. I need a warm fire – I am chilled to the bone.

Warmth embraced Elle as she entered her home. She headed straight for the fire, and stood in front of Stanley's portrait. She removed her hat and shook down her hair, and was suddenly reminded of another friend who she would never see again; Angus Argyle. His death was something she could not comprehend.

Footsore and weary she burst into tears, all pent up feelings rushed to the fore and she embraced the relief they bought.

'Stanley – my dearest friend, I hope you and Angus are enjoying each other's company, and your mother is fussing around you both. I miss you all so very much. My heart beats and yet it is broken. Death and love rip it apart.

Can you imagine I ache to be held in the arms of a man who nigh on destroyed you – who killed your father? Yes, I love Matthew Gant. There I've said it. I love him, heart and soul, I wish he were mine. Foolish? Mayhap I am but I cannot deny love. We parted on bad terms, and sadly society and class will keep us apart. I left a dear friend behind because of this love. Yet again, I mourn the loss of a friend.'

Moving from the main room to her bedroom, Elle took note of fresh linen, and sweet-smelling lavender bags. She entered the kitchen area and smiled at the well-stocked pantry. A far cry from a home she entered three years previous. So few years yet so much had happened to her during that time. Sadly, two things had not let go of her heartstrings, loneliness and longing still remained her companions in 1868.

She pulled back the drapes to expose the large picture windows, and looked out to sea. Not one image inspired her, and for once in her life Elle saw only greys and blacks.

Colour – I need colour back in my life. Black haunts me.

She looked to her easel sitting in the corner, a large blank canvas sat awaiting its mistress but she could give nothing. Elle feared her painting days were over.

***

The following morning Elle opened her pantry and closed the door again. Food did not hold her interest. Outside it threatened rain but the outdoors called to her to take a walk.

Her belly tensed, and she snatched at her hat and coat, maybe inspiration would be found along the way. She headed for the farm with token gifts purchased for Josh and Martha.

Her last encounter with Martha was not the best one but she did need to thank them both for looking after Orris Cottage. The new pipe and lace cap saddened her, and a fragment of resentment hit her. She should have purchased those gifts for her parents, and each time she thought of how they had treated her she hated them for their emotional torment. It was a vicious circle of bewilderment and hurt.

The tension she experienced left the moment Martha opened the door.

'Welcome. Welcome home! Come. Sit.' Martha ushered Elle to a seat at the well-scrubbed table central to the kitchen. Elle pulled off her gloves and memories of Rose serving her a Christmas meal surged into her mind, and for a second Elle needed to catch her breath. She held back another bout of sobbing by looking around at the changes made in the kitchen but still the memories hounded her.

Martha poured creamy buttermilk into a cup and added a drizzle of honey. She handed it to Elle as if a mother comforting a child upon a cold day. A shiver ran down Elle's spine but she drew pleasure in the fact that there were no hard feelings relating to their last meeting. Martha nudged the cup towards Elle.

'You look peaky. Drink up and get the foreign dust out of your bones. Home feeding is what you need my girl. Look at you, skin and bones. Your hair is as dull as the day. The day you chose to come back home was not a day too soon.'

'Thank you, Martha. I am pleased to be home. Paris was fine enough but I have the sea in my blood. They are strange people with their fanciful ways. I learned many a lesson and will always be grateful but Dovercourt is where I want to be from now on, no more travels to foreign lands. It saddens me that Angus succumbed to that dreadful disease, and am thankful you are both well. Thank you both for looking after my home, it was cosy and smelled so sweet, a true comfort. Thank Josh for caring for my herb garden, not a weed choked them. I missed their fragrance.'

'Thank him yourself, Mistress Painter.' Josh's jovial voice entered the room before the man himself, and when he did he sported a large grin and rushed to shake her hand. 'Welcome back, Elle. My goodness, Martha, this girl needs a slice of your bread – only half of her has returned!'

Elle giggled. 'You tease, Josh. I am not so skinny. Admittedly I did not eat as healthily in France. I often skipped meals if painting a commissioned piece.' Elle bit into the bread, chewed and swallowed. She licked butter from her fingers and looked to the plate for another slice.

'Martha, your bread will keep me fed for a week. I have a feeling I will soon be back to my former self, Josh. Now I must leave you both and visit your master. I have business to discuss. Angus left me his worldly goods, bless him, and made Charles Gant my guardian, can you believe my good fortune? It appears I am to become a wealthy young woman. Do you know if Mr. Gant is home?'

Josh nodded his reply. 'Sad day when your friend passed. We have been fortunate this end of town. Sorry for your loss but pleased he saw your future cared for, thoughtful man.'

Elle pulled on her gloves and gave them both a smile.

'It was good to see you both. I will visit again shortly.'

Elle sensed their eyes watching her walk away. It saddened her to know they would never be the close friends she desired back in her life but gave her comfort to know she still had their friendship and they were not folk who held grudges.

She walked with speed towards the large house two fields ahead. The well-walked lane wound its way between dog-rose & bramble hedges. The path was still damp from the previous day's fog and Elle cursed her folly in wearing her delicate French boots. A last gift to herself from France, the square-toed, decorative buttoned ankle boots were not designed for trudging through a country lane – of something her toes were making her painfully aware. To add insult to injury, the first drops of rain descended.

When the house came into sight, Elle gave a sigh of relief. The imposing building looked grand compared to the cramped ones of Paris. Elle stopped to take in the scene and looked upon the freshness that surrounded her, and inhaled the decaying leaf aroma. The rain fell harder and she lengthened her stride along the driveway of the house. Halfway it occurred to her that Matthew might be home, and panic set in.

How can I look at him without declaring my love for him? But is that not the reason you have returned? Stop! Stop arguing inside my head!

Her heart hammered inside her chest, and another large inhalation helped her gain control once again.

Several curtained windows stared back at her, and she frowned. Josh told her they were home but it appeared not the case.

Elle slipped around the side of the property, although she was expected she did not feel comfortable knocking at the ornate front door.

She lifted the latch of the kitchen door, and smiled at both the housekeeper and cook who were enjoying a brief break from duties. Both scrambled to their feet and rushed to greet her.

'Well look what the cat dragged in from the fields. Elle Buchanan back from her travels!' The cook grabbed her arm, and pushed her towards a seat.

'We missed our little chats from when you painted the mistress.' The warm glow of friendship touched Elle. Both women were genuinely pleased to see her. A steaming cup of tea was placed before her.

'Gracious, such a welcome. Oh, and tea, a delightful treat. Thank you.'

'My dear young lady – for you are just that nowadays – look how you have grown. Is that gown from Paris? It is simple but oh so pretty. Pretty in pink, do you not think?' The housekeeper directed her questions at top speed, and Elle giggled as the woman continued with her exclamations.

'Your boots! How petite and exquisite they are – how grubby, too. Daisy!' The housekeeper called to a young maid who appeared from a backroom within seconds.

'Miss. Buchanan's boots are in need of a clean before she enters the master's study – be quick about it. She will drink her tea and wait, so do not dally about your business.'

'Mrs. Saville, you will give me airs and graces above my station with such treatment but thank you.' Elle sipped her tea, and enjoyed the company of the older women.

'Nonsense, you could never have airs and graces, you are too kind-hearted. We know you have had a tough road, Rose hinted when she was alive. She only wants the best for you, and it is up to us to ensure her wishes are carried out. Both Josh and Martha care for you, and I know they missed you greatly. Come and sit, do tell us about your adventures, Elle. We heard snippets from upstairs but nothing about your painting. When I heard he was travelling to France I enquired if your paths would cross but Master Matthew merely mentioned he had seen you, and you were famous in France.'

Elle laughed aloud. She imagined the gossip in the kitchen had been exaggerated.

'Famous in France? Oh dear, I fear he exaggerates. I merely had one painting on show. I did sell it, my tutor fetched a good price for me, and it paid for my journey home. Somewhere I am happy to be once again I hasten to add.

Paris is rather theatrical. There are women – girls, who would bring on the vapours to attract the attentions of the males. Men who wore more frills than the whole of the female population of England I wouldn't wager. I am afraid I confess they were too pretty for me. I like the style of the Englishman, they have a sensibility about them.'

A sudden image of Matthew came into her head, and she felt the warmth of an embarrassed flush spread over her face. Elle, aware she chatted and attracted more attention than she would have liked, took another sip of her tea. She could feel the eyes of the others upon her and hoped her boots were finished. A sudden desire to be out of the house came upon her but she knew she still had to see its master. Relief came in the form of the maid, Daisy. She placed Elle's boots before her, and Elle shooed her away when she attempted to place Elle's foot inside them.

'I must not detain you any longer, Daisy. I am perfectly able to put on my own boots, thank you for your kind offer.' The girl looked to the housekeeper, and Elle watched as she left the room. The housekeeper approached Elle, and with haste Elle put on her boots and secured them.

'You must not spoil me, I will be looking for her in the morning to dress me!' She made light of the affair with a joke, and hoped the housekeeper was not offended by her actions. 'I must see Mr. Gant, please could you tell him I am here. I am certain he will see me if he is not entertaining another.'

'He is in his study. I will let him know you are here. I am afraid the mistress has taken to her bed. Severe headaches bother her, and the daylight appears to aggravate them tenfold, hence the closed curtains in certain rooms.' The housekeeper left the kitchen, and the cook excused herself for being busy with chores. Elle waited patiently.

Please don't let Matthew be home. Please don't let Matthew be home. She repeated the words as if a mantra to be followed religiously. She continued reciting them in her head as she followed the housekeeper upon the announcement she was most welcome in the Gant home, and was to proceed upstairs as soon as possible.

A soft instruction to enter left her face to face with Charles. He wore a tired expression with the smile Elle remembered.

'My dear Miss. Buchanan. Welcome back to England – to Dovercourt. A place that cannot possibly compare to the capital of France but welcomes home its daughter, nevertheless.' He walked around from the back of his desk, and shook her hand.

'My wife is quite unwell I am afraid, and as I suspect it is the business of your trust fund you seek to discuss, I feel my study the appropriate place for us to talk. Please, take a seat.'

Elle sat in the plush green chair trimmed with leather. She watched as Charles pulled out a stack of papers, and flicked through until he found the ones he required. A sniffle from under the table told her his dogs were snug by his feet. Loyal and loving pets to a man who deserved their trust. She felt a loyalty to him, despite their last face to face meeting.

'Thank you for seeing me without notice, Mr. Gant – Charles. It is a sad affair, and Angus has been most generous. Thank you for attending to his needs and requests. It is work that is beyond me. You may have noticed an improvement in my vocabulary and accent but I am afraid that is as far as my life lessons have taken me. Any further improvement would mean long days of tuition.' Elle spoke while he glanced through a set of legal looking papers. She hated the silence between them, it made her mind think of Matthew, and the dreadful mantra chimed in on a regular beat.

'I am sorry to hear of your wife's sickness, and do hope she recovers swiftly.'

Charles laid down the papers, and smiled at her. 'Thank you, she is quite unbearable when she is unwell. Fortunately, she sleeps the majority of the day.'

Elle, embarrassed by his open manner against his wife, said nothing. If truth be known, she cared little about the woman, and the fact she was not around to belittle and rant over Elle's presence, pleased her somewhat.

'Our business is to discuss your inheritance, and the vast collection of paintings you have inherited. I am under instruction to sell all but one of your choosing, and add the money to the cash fund already in your name. Several of the paintings he was commissioned to sell on the behalf of others have been returned to their owners. The more – let us say, risqué ones have been sold on to those who would appreciate them far more than you – or indeed, I might do. You raise an eyebrow, Miss. Buchanan. Surely you – ah, yes, my past snaps at my heels. You have enjoyed the artist's side of the canvas, so to speak. It is in my past, and I appreciate your discretion over the years. I assure you, each and every one of those paintings has been sold. I only own one drawing which makes me flush at the very sight of it, and we both know which one that is, as I have mentioned.'

Charles pinched his lips together, and Elle regretted her reaction to his words.

'Mr. Gant. Forgive me. It was rude of me to doubt the whereabouts of the paintings. You are a man of good word, and as you say, your past is just that, the past. Let us move forward. From today you will call me, Elle, and I will address you as Charles in private. Today I feel a fraud, a cuckoo in the nest. Your staff have treated me as a lady – and we all know that is not the case, and you speak to me as an equal, and again, we know that not to be a truth. I am, however, fortunate to have you as a guardian, and a friend. With regard to Angus's estate, I need your support. For me, it is a sad affair with the joy of returning to my cottage. I confess my feelings are in turmoil for varied reasons. One thing I am certain of, is that you are the one stable person I need in my life – I have no desire to offend you with regards to your past, and nor do I wish to lose your valuable guidance. I need you in my life.'

As she uttered her final words the door to the study clicked shut. The sound startled both of them, and Elle could not recall hearing the door open. Charles rose, opened the door and looked down the hallway.

'Matthew. Don't leave, come see who has returned from Paris. I didn't hear you come home.'

Elle's heart skipped a beat, and danced with a furious thud inside her chest. She suppressed the urge to run, and she soon realised it was too late to do so for Matthew stood a few feet away, and she would have to run through him to get out of the room. He was more handsome than she remembered from their last meeting. His face flushed with evidence of the cool outer air from which he had just left, looked healthier than in the past. He stood with his hands behind his back and stared at her. She could see the darkness in his eyes and they shone as black as those within her painting. It was evident she was not someone he was pleased to see, and he carried a stiffened body to portray his displeasure. His voice was void of personality as he greeted her out of politeness.

'Miss. Buchanan. Welcome back to England.' He didn't offer his hand but walked to a chair beside his father's desk and sat down. All manners and etiquette were greatly highlighted by their absence. Fortunately, Charles's interest was in the papers upon his desk so he failed to see the uncomfortable scene in the room. Elle was grateful to Matthew for not attempting to take her hand as she felt sure she would fall into his arms and beg him to kiss her once again. She longed to be drawn into another lingering kiss.

'Mr. Gant. Thank you, it is a pleasure to be back.' She sat in the remaining vacant chair beside him, and ensured it was not so close they touched.

Charles offered them both a glass of wine. 'Thank you, no; your housekeeper and cook fed and watered me, and I rarely drink wine.'

Matthew snorted out a pretend cough, and she gave him a withering look. Paris was a memory she'd rather forget, and he obviously had not and his snigger was a reminder to torment.

'Forgive me. I was reminded of a lady friend who supped too many glasses of claret. I warned her it could shrivel the …'

He was cut off by his father's sharp voice.

'I have no desire to hear any more of your gutter-like antics …'

Matthew interrupted his father in return.

'Heart – I said it would shrivel her heart, if she'd had one of course.' He turned his attention back to Elle with an all-knowing stare.

'How long will you be staying before your return to Paris?' He politely enquired, the stiffened unfriendliness still evident in his tone but the remains of the snigger held an edge to the enquiring voice.

'I am home for good.' Elle softened her voice, and lowered her head in the hope he would accept it as an apology, to try and convey her need to close the cold gap between them. 'I have all I need here. Paris no longer holds my heart, I ...'

'Quite right. Home where you belong.' Charles voice made her jump as he interjected. She had almost forgotten he was in the room.

'Matthew, I wonder if you will escort Miss. Buchanan to sign papers tomorrow. I have a farm meeting and am unable to get away. Angus's left a few things that need a signature of the recipient of his estate.'

Matthew rose from his seat, his annoyance rippled around the room, and Elle shuddered.

'I am afraid Miss. Buchanan will have to find herself another escort, Father. I too have a meeting. My apologies. Forgive me, I am going to say hello to mother, and will leave you two to tend to whatever business it is that you are guiding Miss. Buchanan through during the time when she *needs you in her life*. Good afternoon to you both.' With the words stinging sharper than a slap, Elle sat iron rod straight, not daring to move. Matthew had heard words between his father and her, and misinterpreted them.

He thinks I love his father! That I have a need for his father!

He pushed back his chair and left the room before his father could respond.

'Unfortunately, I will have to postpone the meeting at the solicitors, Elle. My son attends several meetings to assist with his recovery from nightmares, and drink. I do not wish to detract him from the right path. I will send word for another day. Now, if you could sign here, I will give you the allowance for this month. You will have enough to consider a larger property in the future.'

The thought of leaving Orris Cottage horrified her, and Elle shook her head.

'I will never leave, it is my one true home.'

Charles laughed, and she rose from her seat, his laugh was infectious and she joined him.

'Why do we laugh, sir? Does the thought of me being your neighbour forever, worry you?'

His laugh became louder. 'The very fact you think a husband would want to live in your artist's parlour caught my fancy, I apologise. I meant for you to purchase a family home, for when you wed. A possible dowry.'

Elle stopped laughing. His words hit hard. She had never thought about her future in such a way – married had never been a word in her vocabulary. Since losing Matthew's friendship, as little as it was, she had put all thoughts of a future out of her mind.

'I am never going to marry, Charles. It is not the way forward for me. I will remain a hermit maid, tucked away in my artist's parlour, as you so rightly called it, although I prefer to think of it as my sanctuary. We will arrange another meeting, as you say and until then I wish you well.'

With sadness, Elle walked home. She had hoped to catch a glimpse of Matthew, even an opportunity to express her regret with regard to Paris, unfortunately, he was not to be found. His quip about a wine-drinking woman and her shrivelled heart, hit home. He had dismissed Elle to the ranks of the unsavoury women he once bedded – in all probability still did – either way he had ensured Elle knew there was no longer a place for her in his life.

CHAPTER 29

Death of Love

The funeral cortege moved slowly to the church on the coldest day in March. The elaborate affair did not cost the compulsory five shillings most would have to find to satisfy the strict mourning etiquette, staff of the house concluded it cost more than their combined wages for a year.

Floral tributes lined the church entrance and beyond, and professional mourners wailed for their life's worth. Elle, Josh, Martha, and other members of Charles Gant's staff stood along the church path with heads bowed out of respect for his dead wife. Evangeline Gant succumbed to one headache too many, and suffered a major bleeding brain according to the family doctor.

Upon hearing the news of Evangeline's death, Elle visited Charles to pay her respects – a visit she regretted each day she rose for the past four days. Firstly, seeing Evangeline lying pale-faced and with the strangest crook to her mouth, giving an odd sense to the viewer that she smiled, chilled Elle to the core. The coffin was an extremely ornate affair, and had been set as tradition dictated, in the kitchen area. Elle ventured upstairs to offer condolences, and Matthew's accusation upon her arrival took her breath away with such a vicious wrench, she fought composure over a faint.

Matthew dismissed the housekeeper who escorted Elle, and opened the door to a small parlour. Elle, confused by the obvious anger he expressed in his actions, held back from entering. His hand pushed into the small of her back, and she had no choice but to stumble forward.

'In all that is good w...' Her voice was silenced by his fierce interruption.

'Miss. Buchanan. My mother's sheets are still warm, and I take it you have come to claim her place – such is the *need* for you to have my father in your life. I will pass along your condolences. Feel free to visit and warm his sheets another day, preferably *after* the funeral. I will see you out myself, and ensure you have left the premises. I wish no gossip during our mourning period. Follow me.'

He grabbed her wrist, and Elle stumbled again. She wrenched her arm back, and followed him to the main entrance. The sting of his words chiselled into her heart, and if he had stabbed her with a knife, she knew it would be as painful. Her mind challenged him but her mouth could not express. He pointed outside, and walked away leaving her shaking with shock and rage. She wished her brain would allow her mouth to open and offer him a tongue-lashing in return for his insults. Only respect for the dead woman and her mourners prevented her from doing so, and she continued her silent rants until she reached home.

For over seven hours Elle sobbed. She mourned the death of love – the kind of love she knew she would never find again. Evangeline's heart might have stopped but Elle's had torn in two. No repair could ever heal the wound.

On the day of the funeral, she needed to show Matthew he was wrong with his accusations, and place herself where he could see where she belonged, hence the fact she stood with the staff during their moment of respect. Drops of rain fell amongst them, and murmuring filtered along the line.

'She'll be off to Heaven then.' Martha declared, brushing away the drops from her coat. Elle frowned, not understanding the whispered words.

'Superstition. A good sign for a funeral – or rather the dead awaiting at The Gates.' Josh explained. 'Ah, here comes the master.'

The closer Charles, Matthew, and the men she assumed were relatives of Evangeline came to the end of the line, the more nervous Elle became. She knew Matthew would not create a scene in public, and hoped he understood her presence was out of respect for his mother, and no other motive intended.

Her nervousness exacerbated as the entourage of black clothed mourners stopped in front of her, and Charles put out his gloved hand.

'Miss. Buchanan, thank you for attending. Allow me to introduce you to my wife's brother.'

Elle could not believe her ears, Charles introduced her as if she were someone of great importance.

This is farcical – please leave – move along.

She gave a shy smile at the man and found what she hoped was a sincere voice, fully aware of the many eyes upon her, once set in particular. 'My condolences. Mrs. Gant is a great loss to our community.'

To her great surprise, Evangeline's brother grabbed Elle's hand and shook it heartily.

'I understand you are responsible for capturing the softer side of my sister, in your portrait of her. Thank you. She could be quite dour at times these past few years but underneath there was a young girl with a smile – we just rarely saw it, thank you.' He gave a cold look to his nephew, and it was obvious to Elle, Matthew's uncle resented his nephew's past actions.

Embarrassment of him confiding in her in such a public manner, surged through her body like hot coals. So many faces looked upon hers, and the last thing Elle wanted was attention. She took a side-glance to where Matthew stood. His face spoke more than words could ever do, he was angered by the scene he had just witnessed. His father had selected her from the group, and his uncle gushed over her work and made reference to his mother in an unkind manner. She needed to rectify the moment but she also wanted to punish Matthew for his recent treatment of her. A newfound courage roared inside, and Elle gave a crisp speech.

'Sir. I fear you misinterpreted your sister's ability to conduct herself in a manner perfected for her role. She was someone to be admired. A smile is not always the first thing to seek when you look for good inside a person. Mrs. Gant did not need a smile to show the world she maintained a well-run household. She fiercely defended her marriage, and ensured her son finally followed an honourable path – a veritable triumph for a woman, some might say. She did not need to wear a smile, and indeed, I am certain there were some days when she must have been in too much pain, physically and emotionally, to do so. It was an honour to be asked to paint her portrait.'

Elle drew breath, and prayed her words would be interpreted in the correct manner by those to whom they were directed, Matthew in particular.

The brother-in-law of Charles Gant, gave a gracious nod of his head, and appeared bemused by her words. He opened his mouth to speak but instead moved forward to talk to other members of the mourning congregation. Charles lingered, gave her a puzzled frown and joined the others. Matthew moved in front of her, his glare said it all. He understood her message; his actions of the past could have brought about his mother's headaches. *He* might be responsible for her death, as he had been for Stanley's father. His drinking days were an embarrassment, and took away the smile from his mother's face. Elle had found her target, and the score was settled.

Why don't I feel triumphant? I beat him at his game of hurting another.

She turned away and looked at his family gathering by the church entrance.

'Your family is waiting for you, sir.'

Realising he would have to follow protocol, she raised her hand to shake his, he gave her hand a slight squeeze, and startled her.

'Your eyes captured *her* soul. You left no blank space, in *her* you saw something. May you never lose your talent. The portrait will bring comfort to my father during his years of mourning. The double meaning of his words were not lost on Elle, he repeated words spoken in France. She lowered her head in acknowledgement and acceptance that he still needed her to find light in his eyes. Was it a challenge? She repeated the words in her mind as he walked away.

Did he just insult me again? Hinting about his father's two-year mourning period. Does he want me to find the light in his eyes – does he want me in his life?

Elle stared at his back, strong and upright, and the scene brought back upsetting memories of their fight in

Paris, and of how she watched him walk away.

She waited until all mourners entered the church, and slipped away. The tolling bells clanged out their mournful tune, and each tinny sound beat its way inside her head. She fought the urge to scream, and instead made her way home, where, she promised herself she would concentrate upon her garden and painting. Charles Gant, and his son, would become distant neighbours. She would arrange any legal transactions with relation to her inheritance, away from both homes. Elle no longer wished to become fuel for Matthew's raging fire, nor fodder for the gossipmongers. It was time to reconsider her options, and returning to Paris was one which reared its head over and over during the walk home.

CHAPTER 30

By Demand

Braskell and Son: Solicitors
September 5th 1868

Dear Miss. Buchanan,

Our client instructs that as six months of correspondence, and verbal requests for you to attend Gant's Hall, have failed to gain your attention, it is with regret he now dictates the following:

You are to attend Gant's Hall at thirty minutes past two o'clock, on the day of our Lord; September 6th 1868.

Failure to attend will mean the paintings held in your name, will be destroyed by fire at thirty minutes past four o'clock the same day. Our client has no desire to store the property for longer than is necessary. It is his intention to auction the paintings to secure funding for your future. However, given that you have failed to claim your monthly income, and shown no interest in your inheritance, he intends to relinquish all rights as a guardian.

It is our advice, given the high value of the property that you adhere to his request.

Yours Truly

Tobias Braskell

Elle placed the letter on her dresser. Josh delivered it along with the milk for her breakfast, and she ignored the envelope guessing it was yet another demand for her presence from Charles.

She'd spent the day wandering around her garden and attempted to paint a rose or two but still the inclination to paint failed her. She forced herself to draw birds, plants and anything else that caught her eye but still nothing could lead her to her oils and canvas.

Temptation to pour a sherry from the decanter the letter leaned against was strong but she was not fond of the rich, sweet liquid. She remembered a case of wine purchased from France, and opened a bottle, luxuriating in its flavour. Memory of Jacques friendly reprimand of how one should never drink alone, made her hesitate but only for a few seconds.

No one here will object, and I am in need of relaxation.

She settled in her seat but could not rest. She paced the floor and cursed loudly in French, and damned Charles and his demands. The past six months had been emotional free, and a pleasurable summer spent walking the town, and seaside in search of inspiration, promised to drift into an autumn of much the same. Elle enjoyed her hermit-like state, and her gardens shared the results of her constant attention. She wore a colour on her flesh young women of the day would have declared as unfashionable. Martha stated the peach glow suited her, and she looked the picture of health at last. Elle cared little about her appearance, and her French gowns were stored away, replaced by simple painting smocks and pinafores.

Her dainty boots were wrapped in tissue paper and stored with the gowns, and plain leather slippers adorned her feet in their place. She enjoyed comfort and practicality over fashion. Her many pairs of stockings were hole free, and she ensured she bathed often, aside from that, she no longer cared for silks and satins, and had no reason to dress in the latest fashions. She saw only Josh and Martha on rare occasions, and they took little note of her clothing. It infuriated her that Charles Gant tarnished her personal pleasures with his demands.

She snatched up the letter once again, and raised her glass at Stanley's portrait.

'Burn paintings? He sums up the ignorance of those who have no passion for the arts, Stanley. Burn paintings, whatever next?' She gulped down her wine, and poured another. 'I have no choice but to attend. Botheration and beyond! The man is in mourning, why can he not sit quietly and think about his loss? Why can he not leave me alone? Why am I drinking wine like a mad woman? Charles Gant, that is why!'

Draining the glass of its contents, she paced the floor, all words directed at her friend's portrait. Her voice grew louder the more her temper rose.

'I need to save those paintings. I *must*, they deserved to be hanged not burned.' The comical pun play on words made her giggle but Elle soon found the serious side to her situation most perplexing.

'My dear friend, if I do not attend that meeting I will have condemned the paintings to the fire myself, I will be no better than he. Tomorrow I will take serious stock of my future. My future – will I find love, Stanley, or am I to remain unloved? All I want in life is for someone to live long enough to enjoy the pleasures of true love with me; a love that lives and breathes'. She slumped back into her chair, and sighed.

'What a nuisance that man has become – burn paintings indeed. Just wait until I see him.'

CHAPTER 31

Desperation

With a pounding head and certainly in no mood for justifying nor defending her reasons for ignoring previous summons, Elle prepared for the meeting with Charles.

She pulled out one of her prettier gowns, a simple affair in autumnal shades, and tugged on her best walking boots with great resentment. To be barefoot and alone is all she desired, not to be trussed up in a manner society expected from a young woman. Elle grinned to herself, she was far from the usual young women of her era. She had money, owned a home and lived a comfortable life – free from the restraints placed upon some young women of the town. Their nannies and mama's would have bouts of the vapours if they were to take a peek through Elle's windows some days. With the desire to paint still at bay, her charcoal etching became the distraction she needed, and black smears were worn on regular basis. They smothered her clothing until she looked more like a child who swept chimneys rather than a young woman creating something artistic.

'Here I go, Stanley. Time for battle. I will rescue the paintings and be home before the hour is through. Wish me luck.' She smiled up at her friend's portrait, and pulled on matching bonnet and gloves, she stepped outside, inhaled the smoke-tinged sea air, and ambled at a leisurely pace to the big house. Despite the annoyance of being forced out of her new routine for the visit, Elle enjoyed the walk.

The bleakness had a beauty of its own, and she loved the area for its rough edges. No fancy architecture graced the pitted pathway, no townsfolk promenading in all their finery graced this side of the beach, only nature at its most basic, and Elle gained an inner peace in the place she called home. No more foreign shores for her, Earlham's beach and surrounding bay had her by the heart and soul.

Upon her arrival at the large house, she hesitated at the front door and deliberated whether to take her usual route via the kitchen. She reminded herself she was summoned to call and had every right to be received as a guest. With a deep breath she pulled the bell.

Invited to sit in the reception area of the hallway while the young servant who answered the door went in search of his master, Elle had time to look around at the many paintings on view, she rose to inspect several masterpieces that captured her interest. Evangeline's portrait now sat in pride of place rather than in the parlour where it originally hung, and Elle looked to her in a different light. Not at how she had painted the woman but of how Evangeline's personality altered over the years, according to her brother.

You had life knocked out of you. Was it an affair he had, or your son's wayward past? I imagine you were different before marriage. I wonder if I am wise to remain on the shelf, I could not bear it if marriage were to stifle the smiles out of me.

'At last you grace us with your presence.' Charles Gant startled Elle, and she swung around but before she could gather her thoughts and give him a piece of her mind, he continued speaking.

'Your face speaks a thousand words, I see you are annoyed by my request you attend the meeting today. It is for your future, now come to the study and we will work through the portfolio together.'

Elle had no choice but to follow him and fancied his mood was as fired up as hers, judging by the way he strode straight-backed down the corridor and into his study.

On his table sat many papers, and Elle knew she would be sitting in front of him for more than the few minutes she originally intended. He sat at his seat and she sat opposite, he said nothing and it irritated Elle, she watched as he flicked through papers and put them into two separate piles. She gave an audible sigh. For want of something to say, Elle decided to dive straight into a conversation, not giving him a chance to reply.

'I see you are well prepared and it is obvious we have a momentous task ahead. I take it these are the records of Angus's paintings? I am here to save paintings not to give into your demand I visit. This is a house of mourning and I am surprised you entertain ideas of business. I left you both alone to adjust to your life without wife and mother, it appears I offended or upset by doing so. My apologies. I spend very little money and did not need extra funds therefore not needing to disturb the household. You …'

Charles arm slammed onto his desk and his inkwell threatened to jump free. Elle, scared by the angry voice he turned upon her, stood up but changed her mind and sat down again. Charles leaned across his desk, and she dared not move. His voice was so loud his dogs slunk from under the desk and moved to the other side of the room where they stood on guard. Their master needed their attention.

'For goodness sake stop your chatter. What I do in my own home is my business. I mourned the loss of my wife the day your friend's father was killed and my useless son ruined ours. You sit here behaving like a woman of substance when in fact all you are is a guttersnipe who can paint. How dare you suggest I demanded you visit, I merely need to settle your affairs before leaving for India. I have but one week to dispose of the paintings thanks to your reluctance to do as I asked. If we may get on with the task in hand?'

Charles sat back down, his deep-creased brow settled from a frown to that of calm, and Elle relaxed into her seat.

'India? You are taking a holiday in India?'

Charles grunted as his concentration returned to the two piles of paper.

'Not a holiday. I inherited my father's large plantation, coffee was his trade. His brother passed away shortly after my wife, and it became my responsibility. I have decided to spend my last years in warmer climes.'

Elle's inner clock stopped ticking. She dared not say a word for fear of what might be released from her mouth. For some strange reason she wanted to scream, to kneel in front of him and beg that he stayed. Charles Gant was the one constant thing in her life, the only one she could turn to in times of trouble. Despite avoiding him all summer, she knew he was there should she be in need of support, and now he was to leave. The loss of another friend felt like a physical blow. Then came a realisation that hit her harder than any physical force could do and if she stood she knew her knees would buckle, a weakness overcame her senses. Her body trembled.

Matthew. I will never see him again.

Her throat closed against the words she wanted to express. No words could share the shock she experienced with Charles's statement. As of next week she would be alone with no opportunity of expressing the love that brewed deep inside. She needed to speak with Matthew before it was too late. If he shunned her at least she would know she had tried to win him over.

She steadied herself against the arms of the chair and rose. Her head had a stuffiness about it and Elle needed air, to inhale the freshness of outdoors. She cleared her throat and composed herself.

'I wish you well, and safe travels. It must be quite an undertaking. Please, sell the paintings and use the money as you wish, give it to a local family in need. You are right. I am nothing more than a child from the gutter who gained airs above her station, but it is only fair you accept some responsibility for my rising in the ranks, so to speak. You have encouraged my art, and agreed to support me on behalf of Angus. I will work to survive, as is fitting for the daughter of working class. I will trouble you no more. One thing I ask, is Matthew home? I have a message from my friend in France to pass along to him.' She hoped her face would not give away her feelings or her white lie. Time was not on her side, and she needed to move on with her life before emotions dragged her to dark depths of despair.

'Elle, I apologise for my outburst. I am under a lot of pressure and you bore the brunt of the explosion. Forgive me? Please, forgive me. You deserve to be where you are today. I have watched you work hard and strive for a better life. A life that has kicked you down several times over. My son is in the stables, he is instructing a new stable hand. I will sell all paintings, and ensure the funds are sent to you, I will however, donate to a family in your name.

Again, I apologise and hope our paths will cross again. I will never sell my drawing and will think of the little waif who found her way into my world, and grew into the kind young woman I see before me. Do allow me to write of my travels and new life, and send me word of those I leave behind.'

Elle said nothing but gave him a small smile, words were not required. She held out her hand and shook his and before she gave into an impulse to hug him, she walked away.

***

Matthew's hands worked with speed as he rubbed down the flanks of his horse. Elle stood back and watched as his arm muscles rippled while he worked. She had never seen him in such a state of undress, and her heart beat a tune she was convinced he would hear. From behind the stall door she fantasised she was the horse, and Matthew's hands stroked her flesh with such tenderness. The very thought flushed a warmth into her belly, this was a new stage in her life, a time to declare love.

'Can I help, Miss?' A stable boy approached Elle, his face glowed with the warmth of exertion. She cursed him inwardly but gave her best smile to the eager-faced child.

'I am in search of Mr. Matthew Gant, and his father told me he could be found instructing the new stable hand. Would that be yourself?' She teased the lad wanting to win him over. Her pretence of not being able to find Matthew would not have gone unnoticed, the man stood only feet away. Meekness and mild manners were to be her distraction.

'I fear I am quite at a loss as to where I might find your master. I was about to ask the groom over there.' She lifted her head to Matthew's direction, grooming his horse and still without his outer coat, his shirt sleeves rolled high over flexing muscles.

'I will fetch him for you, miss. That is Mr. Matthew. He likes to care for Isabel himself. A kind man to his horse.' The boy ran through the small yard and to Matthew. Elle continued to stare at the man she loved, she captured every move to store away for future memory moments. She sighed with longing.

Lucky Isabel.

Elle toyed with her gloves while she waited for him to come to her. She saw him rinse his face and hands at the pump, and put on his coat. Courage nigh on left her but she vowed to herself he would know her true feelings within the next few moments.

'Miss. Buchanan. I take it my father is still alive and you did not burn him at his own stake. How I would have liked to hear your response to his summons and declaration of intent to burn your paintings.' Matthew played the politeness well in front of the boy. He dismissed him with the firmness of a kind master, and the boy ran to continue his chores.

'A pleasant child.' Elle said.

'A worker, I'll grant him that much. Loves the horses, and that is in his favour. Can we establish you are not here for my father, about my father or to admire the stable boy?' Matthews's voice took on a serious tone and Elle faltered.

'I um, I f ...' She twisted her gloves in her hand. 'I came to say goodbye. Your father tells me you are moving to India. It would be impolite of me to not say farewell.'

Tell him, Elle. Tell him.

'Indeed the house is in packing hysteria since my father announced the move abroad. He intends to sell the house you know, eventually, if all goes well on the plantation.' Matthew stared over her head, and Elle was grateful they did not make eye contact. Courage still failed her in her intended task.

'Oh. He never mentioned selling the property. I naturally assumed the staff would remain and run the place. Without a master in residence and with no intention of returning, I suppose your father is wise in his decision.'

Tell him, Elle. Tell him.

Matthew looked down at her, a small crease formed between his eyes and across his nose. Elle turned away, she could not maintain his stare. She looked to the horse nearby.

'You will be busy yourself no doubt – with packing.' Matthew said but his voice had a sarcastic tinge to it and Elle looked at him in puzzlement.

'Packing? I fail to understand you, packing? Why would I be packing?'

'India. No doubt you will head off for India to warm my father's bed. Away from prying eyes and the mourning restrictions, you both would enjoy the freedom to *enjoy* each other's company.'

Elle allowed her hands to drop by her sides, she feared if she raised them she would strike out and slap at his face. He still thought she and his father were lovers, and she desperately needed him to stop and listen, to know the truth yet something held her back.

If he loved me, he would never think those things about me. He would not torment me. You have to let go, Elle. Let him go.

'Frankly I am beyond words, Matthew. Time again you accuse me of warming your father's bed, and time again I have denied it, doing nothing but telling you the truth. Your father has been good to me and supported me in times of need. Never have we betrayed your mother or her memory. You need to look elsewhere for another to tease and heap cruel assumptions upon. I hope your journey will be a pleasant one. Forgive me for walking away and stating I hope I never lay eyes upon you again. You are an unkind man with a sharp tongue, you wound people who deserve less. You take pleasure in serving up painful embarrassments. Goodbye to you, and might I add, good riddance.'

The lane and fields held little interest as she walked home. Her face, damp with tears, grew cold with the tidal winds blowing from the north. Elle cried for the loss of love and with anger that once again she failed to tell Matthew her true feelings. She replayed the scene over and over, and concluded it was time to put him out of her mind. With him in India, and no need for her to visit the house, life would become less complicated. Time would heal the hurt he seared upon her heart. She would need time to heal, a long time but at last she had the urge to paint, inspiration struck when she saw him with Isobel.

CHAPTER 32

1869 – Rejection

Springtime threw a party of colours around the fields. The meadows bloomed with wild flowers, and silver-tipped birch trees with their elegant canopies dripped with catkins. Wild anemones and wood sorrel sat beneath the shade of the downy trees while sunrays dappled the ground.

Elle watched as Josh and a group of young men from the town lifted fencing in place. The ewes and their young were being introduced to the front pastures and it was time to watch them skip and jump their way to freedom. Overwintering in sheds bought about a sense of release, and Elle felt she understood them as they ran bleating while under the careful watch of a sheepdog.

Only the day before had she run barefoot along the sand, her hair down and the sun warming her shoulders. Six months had passed since she last saw Matthew and Charles, and an intense period of artistic release was now at an end. Today there was a celebratory feel to the air, and Elle was in the mood to celebrate.

'When you've finished there, could you tend to the side fields, Josh? It is time to bring out the calf, he needs to roam and his mother is in need of a feed, the grass is fresh over there. 'Josh raised his hand and waved in acknowledgement.

When the big house and surrounding land went on the market, Elle approached the legal representative and purchased the property.

She wandered through every room and envisaged Matthew doing the same in the past. Her mind told her to not purchase and to walk away but her heart pulled her closer, so close she knew it the only way she could heal.

Orris cottage became her studio, and many aspiring artists paid for regular lessons. Elle was a wealthy woman, and ensured local people were treated fairly when working for her, she was a well-respected employer.

She took advice from Josh and local farmers and set up the best fields for livestock, and added to the quota Charles left with the property.

Inside the house she furnished it with simple colours but filled the walls with vibrant paintings. Stanley had pride of place in the main room, and her more recent pieces shone out in a newly created gallery. Today she would arrange for her latest work to sit upon a central easel, content all demons who prevented her from painting in the past were now released, and her creativity was once again at its peak. In a month or so she intended to host a public viewing.

'Excuse me, ma'am, there is a group of travellers asking for work, and when there are more than three I know you like to deal with employment instructions. I've sent them around the back yard.' Elle looked at the young girl she employed, a doe eyed girl who doted upon her mistress. Elle saved the girl from the workhouse by all accounts.

'Thank you, Jane. I will attend to them in a few moments. Tell cook to serve them soup and bread, and anyone in need of new clothing, ensure they receive it.'

Elle's reputation as a kind employer was spreading and many knocked upon the door looking for a day's work. She insisted all were given one day to earn a coin, receive a meal, and have their personal needs attended to in the form of washing or repairing their clothes. Her staff were horrified at first but soon learned to carry out her instructions and protect their mistress from harm. One or two rogue navvies had tried their chance with snatching a kiss, and were swiftly dealt with by her loyal servants.

It took a few weeks for her to recognise they looked to her as a lady of means, and she ensured she conducted herself as best she could while at the house. When in her studio she relaxed and stripped herself of all finery. Her life balanced well, and all who were part of it were content.

She slipped downstairs to the kitchen, and smiled when she saw her staff attending to the travellers, as she picked up a jug of buttermilk a woman caught her eye.

Mother!

Elle looked frantically around the yard, and sure enough, there was her father and the way he lolled around, she knew he had supped more than his fair share of ale that day. Her hand trembled with the jug in jeopardy of falling to the floor.

They cannot see me. I do not need them in my life. But they are my parents. What am I to do?

Martha came into the kitchen, and took the jug from her hands, Elle sat down at the large table and put her head in her hands.

'Whatever is the matter child, you look so frightened?' Martha and Josh had taken Elle under their wing when she shared plans of her future at Gant's hall, and she left them to assist with the running of the place. Both knew her history, and Elle had been tempted to confide in Martha about Matthew but decided she needed to keep that snippet of information to herself.

'You see the two by the water barrels?' She pointed out the two people she referred to, and Martha nodded.

'They are my parents. I recognised my mother first, and my father didn't need pointing out, he has drunk a few too many. The men should be aware as he used to enjoy a fist fight if ever there was an opportunity. Often he would create the chance. My mother is a cat when it comes to clawing her way out of a situation and into the next, I need them gone, and today. Josh and the boys should be summoned. I will move amongst the party and see if they recognise me, all staff must call me Mistress Gant. No questions, and no slip ups. The minute that pair get to know it is me, this place will be stripped out for money to spend at the tavern. He is my father and will claim his right to lord it over me, believe me.' Elle rushed her whispered words, and ushered Martha out of the door before the woman could reply. Elle watched as she instructed a young boy to run and fetch Josh.

This ought to be a joyous occasion. I should be embracing there return. How can I not feel love?

Elle patted her hair into place, and stepped into the yard. She whispered to each member of her staff they were to call her by her assumed name, she warned there would be dire consequences for all if her request was not carried out. She picked up a warm shawl, and walked over to her mother. The woman's hair moved with lice, and Elle shivered with disgust. Drink had taken its toll on them both but Elle suppressed the sympathy that would normally rise for a stranger in such a position.

'Take this, it will help during the cool evenings. I have a man's jacket that will suit you, sir.' She addressed her parents as politely as she would any other in the yard. Her father wiped away drool from his chin and chewed on the slice of ham offered by her maid.

'Got any ale, wench?' Her father said and followed it with a belch.

Her mother cackled at his audacity, and snatched at the shawl.

'Fine wool. Look, my lover, a toff's shawl for me but no ale for you.'

Elle cringed at the familiar name her mother used on her father, it bought back a rush of bad memories, and her temper rose.

'We serve only buttermilk.' She retorted in a sharp, authoritative voice. 'I offer food, drink and work for one day. It goes to those who are not inebriated. Sadly, you both fall short of the rules, and I ask that you both move along to the next farm. You will be given a basket of food, and money to tide you over for a few days but I cannot offer you work. Josh and the team will escort you from my premises.'

Elle's breath came in short bouts, her parents did not recognise her, and all they worried about was ale. Her father bleated out his insults.

'You lardy da toffs are all the same. Money but no heart. We've had a hard life and you look down on us.' Another belch escorted his words.

'What my man says is true. You rich folk don't care about us. Your children live with the best in their belly, our daughter, God rest her soul, died of starvation.' The woman made a sign of the cross, and Elle snatched at her hand.

'Get out. Get off my land. If you had a daughter die of starvation my mind tells me she had a lucky escape. Drunkards for parents is not something I wish upon any child. Leave and never show your faces here again, I will have the dogs set upon you. Understand? You are not welcome here, ever.'

Elle said her words through gritted teeth. Never had she felt such contempt for two people in her life. She assumed she was the daughter they claimed had died but it did cross her mind she might have had a younger sister, and her hatred for her parents gained new heights. They stood firm and refused to budge, and she pulled at her mother's arm dragging her across the yard to the main gates, her father staggered behind hurtling insult after insult at Josh who had him by the collar.

'Josh, follow this pair in the cart, and do not let them stop for a drink. Move them on for two miles – or more, do not give them a lift just let them walk.'

Her parents, still ranting their woes and demanding ale, walked ahead while Josh climbed onto the cart with two field workers either side.

Josh shook his head. 'Are they worth our time?' He whispered.

'No but I want them gone from here and they can walk away, they did it once before and this time I can watch them with no regrets or pain. They are two drunkards with no inkling of who I am. Today I am free of them, they will no longer haunt me. Not once did they say they came searching for their daughter, they only declared me dead and demanded ale.'

Elle watched the group leave the end of the lane, and turned to pay attention to those she felt worthy of her care.

CHAPTER 33

Contact and Comfort

Assam Gant Plantation
Assam
India

May 1868

Dear Elle,

My sincerest thank you for your letter, and news of what was once my home. I cannot tell you how much it delights me. Matthew expresses his congratulations via this letter, he was somewhat bemused by the news but content enough to know his old home is in capable hands, as am I.

I am sorry to hear of your parental loss. You are quite right to not allow emotion rule your head. Had they came in search of you, it would have been a different matter. It is my wish you find comfort in the fact you carried out the actions of a daughter pained. To have found kindness in Josh and Martha, gives me comfort. They are good people and I am reassured you will be well cared for – as they are by you.

Life here is very different, and my headaches with the challenges set before me. Coffee plantations are now converted to tea plantations due to a blight and for some reason was named, Devastating Emily.

It is obvious my uncle failed in his duty and let the plantation dwindle to nothing but overgrown fields. I cannot tell you how the project of transforming this place has affected me. I feel alive and as if I have found my calling. The plantation residents are hardworking and deserve a master who will look out for them. I have arranged education for their children, and their living quarters are greatly improved, although I do have plans for extending into the next plantation which grows cotton, and the accommodation there is of higher quality.

Sadly, Matthew does not share my enthusiasm, and suffered bouts of dark depression. He wandered aimlessly around the land and it became of great concern to me. What I enjoy was his burden and not something he should have to endure. My heart-strings tugged harder than I thought when he left, but I do know it is for the best. His intention is to travel, to find something of interest along the way. He confessed an equestrian life is something he wishes to consider, and will travel by train from India to Marseille. This I believe, is to enable him to plan his ideas, learn various techniques in each country he visits and eventually settle in France.

I doubt I will ever see my son again but am at peace knowing he has finally decided to stand on his own two feet.

Please keep me informed of your latest herd, and ideas. If I can be of any help with advice, please write and I will do my best.

Stay safe
Your friend
Charles.

Elle folded the letter and placed it into her pocket. She took comfort in the fact that Charles was happy but the news of Matthew distracted her. When he lived in India she could hold his memory at bay but with him in France, it brought to the forefront their argument in Paris, and awakened a yearning to see him once more.

For days she deliberated handing over the workload of the house and farmland to Josh, and move back to Paris. She wrote to Jacques but burned the letter. Her mind was in turmoil, and she became unsettled. She went in search of a world map, and traced what she thought might be his journey. She asked sailors at the docks how long they fancied it would take from one destination to the next. Matthew and his travels became an obsession until

Martha took her to one side, and reality of her situation became clear.

'You worry me, Elle. Mr. Gant has confirmed he is in good health according to what you read to us, why worry about his son? Both men are of strong stock, and if the younger one can find something in life to focus his wandering mind, then it can be nothing but a good outcome. You my dear, must look to the running of this place, and your students. Art that is where you should concentrate your mind. Upon your future, not the past. Forgive me for being so outspoken but the words have to be told as I see it, and as Josh pointed out, we are the only folk to watch over you now.'

Elle reassured her friend all was well, and stored her maps and paraphernalia away, only pulling them out when a melancholy overcame her mind, and she wanted to share Matthew's journey once more.

CHAPTER 34

Unveiled Love

Many days Elle spent wondering if she had been cruel with turning her parents away. It cost her sleep, and Martha berated her for caring too much as they prepared for the viewing party that evening. Elle did not add that her nights were also spent dreaming of Matthew, and of how she wished to pack her bags and seek him out. She stood listening to her friend, knowing her words were wise and truthful.

'They showed their true colours, Elle. As you said at the time to Josh, they never came in search of you, they never enquired of your whereabouts. They were here for selfish reasons. We will never be your parents, and we have had our falling out but I do hope we have shown you more love than that pair. You had a lucky escape. Look at you, a beauty both in face and heart. This is your night to shine do not let them dull your light.'

Elle moved around the table and pulled Martha into her arms. She allowed the tears to fall. Martha didn't move and both parted with a gentle awkwardness, neither woman was used to showing or receiving affection but that moment sealed a common bond, both wanted to be loved. One by a mother, and one by a daughter she could never conceive.

Martha cleared her throat. 'This won't do, won't do at all. We have food to prepare, and you have a bath to enjoy. Jane has taken the water to your room. Go, shoo, and do not return. We have everything in order, and it is out of your hands until your guests arrive.'

Elle leaned in and gave Martha another hug.

'Thank you. Thank you for everything.'

She left the room and peeked into the viewing gallery. Several pieces were still covered in dustsheets and were to be revealed to the world that evening. Invitations were sent to anyone who Elle felt might have an interest in her work. She had also sent word to Jacques. Since her return she had written letters informing him of her life, and of how she thrived in England. Sadly, he never replied but Elle refused to give up on their friendship.

She climbed the stairs and stopped at the picture she kept back from Angus's collection. He had captured her with hair flowing in the fields of Flatford. Wide-eyed and innocent was scribbled upon the back of the canvas, and he had painted her in just that fashion. Elle showed off the painting for no other reason than it was a memorable day for her, and Angus had painted it and she kept it as a memory to be treasured.

Jane scuttled around Elle's bedroom fussing over the lilac silk gown that hung, newly pressed, on the wardrobe door. It was the first time Elle commissioned a dressmaker to create a gown, and certainly the first one purchased in England. When she lived in Paris it seemed an acceptable thing to do as she replaced her stolen belongings but in her hometown it was an act of pure indulgence. Martha told her it was stuff and nonsense, and if she felt so bad about owning a purpose made gown, replace one of the ones she already owned by giving one away.

Elle took note and gave Jane and Martha choice from her Parisian collection. She arranged with the dress maker to alter them, and both were to be at her side for the momentous evening. This was Elle's coming out event. The day she launched herself as an artist in England, a day she and Angus had discussed would be part of her future, and she needed friends around her in his absence. Josh received instructions to purchase a new suit, and to have the bill sent to Elle.

With only moments until the first of the guests were due to arrive, Elle slipped on her new satin slippers.

As she walked past her image on the stairs she reflected upon how far she had come, and in such a short space of time. Nerves no longer held her firm and she looked forward to a new start in life. Tonight her creativity would be on show, and out for criticism but she did not mind, it was meant to be. This was the path she had strived to reach and tonight was her night. She smiled at Josh standing so erect and stern as he greeted people at the door, and Martha ushered the ladies to the room set aside for them to remove their coats and cloaks. Voices filled the usual silent home and Elle absorbed the atmosphere. It was not one she would enjoy happening every day but for this night the party-like happiness had its place.

She mingled with local business men and their wives, smiling outwardly and giggling inside. Not one knew her background and all assumed she was a wealthy orphan. When asked where here parent's hailed from, she simply said they had been born in Parkston but were no longer with her, indicating they were dead. And they were as far as she was concerned. Anyone asking more questions than she was comfortable in responding to were ushered toward a painting and a new conversation took place.

Satisfied all who had been invited were present, Elle walked to the central easel.

'Ladies and Gentlemen.' She called out above the many voices. 'It gives me great joy and pride seeing you all here this evening. My time studying in France taught me many things, and one of them was that our paintings bring out emotions we cannot express verbally. I once painted a piece called, *Feaux de L'amour - Love Lights*.

It shared those who touched my life in many ways, and the eyes held *my* feelings for them. The painting was sold and I have no regrets for it did not show the truth as I now know it. My new piece is titled *Undeniable Love,* and it gives me great pleasure to share with you tonight.'

Elle pulled away the dustsheet and revealed the image of Isabel, Matthew's horse. In the centre of her body was a pair of eyes, and lights of many shades burst from their centres. The light stream touched a pair of hands – one female and one male – bound by a wreath of seaweed upon which were painted prominent buildings relating to Harwich, a soft haze surrounded them, and the gasps from the ladies of the room told her she had captured love enough for it to be portrayed.

Applause rippled around the room, and a surge of bodies wanting to offer their congratulations formed around her. Elle nodded and smiled in the right places but all the time her eyes were upon the critics who stood in front of the easel. For the first time that night, she panicked.

Have I got it right? Will they understand? The women saw the romantic side but is that enough? Do I want them to see more? To see my desire?

'Bravo'. A voice whispered in her ear. She swung around and faced her French friend.

'Jacques. You came!' She exclaimed.

Her friend gave a sweeping bow.

'It was time for the healing. I was tres curieux. Has the Elle shared her lights, I asked myself. I came to England to celebrate you. I carry secrets with your man, Joshua. We stay at guest house but watch from distance for two days. Surprise for you, non?'

'Surprise? Yes indeed, Jacques. A wonderful surprise, and it is, I stay; *I* stay at a guest house. We will improve your English whilst you are here. Now come, I need to hear your comments about my latest work. Do you approve?'

Elle tugged him away from the dwindling group with an apologetic smile and a promise to return once she had received her visitor from France officially.

'Did *you* see it? Tell me, did you see the light?' She implored. He was the only man in the room who would see what she tried so desperately to share. By allowing her feelings to sink into the canvas she was able to breathe once again, to put Matthew behind her.

'I saw something – not all your lights were shining that day but you showed us more than the love of a horse.' Jacques chuckled.

'But why could you not see all of my lights shining. Why? You of all people should have seen them. They are there – go have another look.' She begged Jacque who shook his head with an apologetic smile.

'I could look at it touts le jour – every day but the lights are not mine to see, they are his. I see your home, and your love of home but the love light is for him to find.'

'Whose? Who do you think my lights shine for, Jacques? You told me once I held back. Say his name – paint his lights, you told me. Have I completed the lesson?' Elle continued to badger her friend with her questions. She snatched at a tray of champagne, offered her friend his glass and sipped at hers. She pulled him closer to the painting, and addressed the room. She raised her glass high.

'To *Undeniable Love* subtitled, *Who does my light shine for?*'

'I think it shines for me.' The voice behind her vibrated along her spine, and her breath caught in her throat. She turned around and faced the man she loved. He'd come back to her, the tender way he spoke, the way he looked at her, it all spoke volumes. He was home, back where he belonged. She looked to Jacques who sported a wide grin. She understood his English had been perfect when he spoke the word, we.

She grasped at Matthew's arm. It was now or never, and while applause filtered around them, she looked at him, soaking up all she loved about him.

'You saw it? You really saw it?' She pleaded with Matthew, the shock of him standing in the room not quite knocking out the anxiety that he might not have seen what was hidden in the painting.

'Yes. In Isabel's eyes I see a tiny vision of me. She loves and trusts me, and you showed me your love through her eyes, you painted a miniature of me, a white image in the dark of her eyes. I'm sorry, Elle. Sorry for everything. I love you, and always have. I was scared of my feelings and now I see I needed to look a little deeper to find yours.'

Elle gave him a coy smile. He had seen it, he had seen her love. Now she had to make him feel it, and that was a future she looked forward to as he pulled her close and their lips healed the past.

THE END

ACKNOWLEDGEMENTS

To my beta readers – you know who you are, and have my undying love for your support.

To those I love – my family and dear friends, thank you for encouraging me forward to obtain my goal.

To my readers – thank you, thank you!

Where I gleaned information and gained inspiration:

Memories via my mother Joan, and father (Gerald Samuel Honeycombe ♥ ~ RIP)

The Harwich Society

Harwich and Dovercourt ~ a time gone by …

Book cover design: Anastasia Publishing Europe / Harwich / by Author

ABOUT THE AUTHOR

Shortlisted: Festival of Romance Fiction
2014: New Talent Award

Glynis Smy, (nee Honeycombe), was born and raised in the coastal town of Dovercourt, near Harwich, in the county of Essex, England.

Her short stories, poetry and articles have been published in various places, in both the UK and Cyprus. Her books have sold worldwide, and reached Amazon bestseller in the historical romance listing, February 2014.

She married her school sweetheart, Peter, in 1979 and they produced three amazing children, Darren, Nicola, and Emma.

When she is not tapping at the keyboard she makes greeting cards to sell for charity and enjoys a spot of cross-stitch or fishing.

Meet and Tweet with Glynis: @GlynisSmy
Facebook Page: Glynis Smy
Author Blog: Glynis Smy

MORE BOOKS BY AUTHOR

Ripper, My Love
Ripped Genes
Maggie's Child
Amazon UK #1 #3 best-seller listing
Victorian Romance Feb / May 2014
Amazon UK #25 top 100 paid listing
Historical Romance Feb 2014
Second round: Amazon Breakthrough Novel
Award 2014

Christmas Scrubs – 2014 Kindle
Medical romance Chick Lit short story

MAGGIE'S CHILD
Chapter 1
Monday 13th October 1856

Intense pain ripped through Maggie's body in waves. Sweat lay on her brow, and nausea drained her. She bit hard on the stick between her teeth. As she entered her sixth hour of labour—the longest pain of childbirth endured by Maggie—she convinced herself death must be around the corner for her and the baby. In past pregnancies, labour was over within two hours, and the babies slithered wearily down the birth canal. All died within the first few minutes of arrival. This, her fifth pregnancy, seemed different. Unable to pinpoint as to why, Maggie concentrated on the task ahead.

Her body, sapped of energy, gave in to nature. Maggie drew in a deep breath, arched her back, and pushed through the pain. Now came the moment she dreaded, the split seconds when life and death merged. When body and soul would cry out with the pain of loss. Bearing down, she bit deeper into the stick. Never had she felt so alone and helpless.

Damn you, Stephen Avenell. Damn your promises.

A breeze wafted across her face, and Maggie welcomed the cool offering. She placed trembling fingers between her legs, and her hands recoiled when she touched a warm, sticky mass.

With speed, she made out a rounded mound, and with slippery hands helped the tiny body into the world. She tugged gently, and while she wrapped her hands around the small mass, a hand grasped at her fingers.

Maggie inhaled and held her breath for a few seconds; the wet hand had a firm grip. Tiny fingers moved and told her there was hope.

She pushed away the stick with her tongue. The wood left behind earthy flavours. Maggie longed to rinse away the taste, but there were no luxuries surrounding her at this delivery. She spat indelicately onto the ground beside her and, with as much speed as she could muster, pulled the babe onto her belly.

With one arm supporting the child, she forced her body downwards and pushed out the afterbirth. With her free arm, she wiped herself clean with rags laid out in readiness.

Now came the moment of truth. Slowly she lifted her head and looked down at the squirming pink flesh that celebrated life on her abdomen. A sob caught in the back of Maggie's throat when a small squeak escaped from rosebud lips. The cries of her baby were an orchestra to her ears. She had never heard a sound from her labours before today. The vibrations against her breastbone were like church bells on a wedding day for Maggie. A sound to be rejoiced.

She cut the cord with a clean knife from her basket, rubbed the child clean with a rag, and bound a binder tight around the rotund belly. Exhaustion kept her lying on the ground. She comforted the child upon her body with one hand while, with the other, she fumbled and wrapped the afterbirth in the bloodied rags. Maggie put them to one side and reached out with trembling hands to hold her new-born for the first time.

The warmth of its skin made hers tingle.

A red face settled to baby pink when she enclosed her arms around its tiny frame and rested it gently in the crook of her arm. She traced her fingers around the mouth and down the cheeks. Eyes opened and looked into hers. Maggie's whole being surged with powerful love as she looked back into them. Tears streamed down her face and ran along the soft downy head of a blue-eyed boy.

She had a son. Baby Sawbury had a mother. Two lives from one body was the only miracle Maggie had ever asked God to grant her. The only child who had managed to find solace in her womb and lived was now telling the world the good news at the top of his lungs.

Sadness crept into her soul when Maggie remembered what was to be done before nightfall. The task to be carried out would be the hardest task of her life. For nine months, she played the role of the happy pregnant woman, despite knowing she would never keep the child. Jacob had been fooled into believing the child was his once she suspected she was pregnant with her lover's baby. Her husband showed no interest, claiming he would only be happy if she produced a boy, live and kicking. Maggie knew that whether boy or girl—if the child lived—Jacob would play no part in his or her life. Telling him was a ploy to protect her and the baby's future. Now that the time had arrived, it was a nightmare—not the plan she had thought simple to carry out. In her heart of hearts, she had convinced herself this baby would die like his siblings.

Now he lived, she needed to face the consequences.

Time was of the essence, and Maggie moved quickly. She spoke to the baby in soothing tones while she wrapped him in linen robes. 'I made these, little one. Your mama made these for you. Every stitch holds my love.'

They were nothing like the delicate outfits she had made for her first born and those who followed. These were simple garments with no embroidery, no identifying motif, but it lifted her spirits to think that at last, the tiny items she had kept secret were to be worn. Maggie would treasure this moment forever. She stopped rushing and gave herself a minute to enjoy her son. To absorb and make a memory of the most joyous event in her life. A twittering yellowhammer flew overhead, and Maggie fantasised it was telling the animal kingdom of a special arrival. Looking down at her son, she marvelled at his perfection and traced a loving finger over his tiny button nose. Both she and Stephen had narrow noses. Maggie's was petite with a slight tilt to the tip. Stephen's was longer. Someone once described it as a Roman nose. The baby's had a stubby shape, fortunately nothing that could be linked with either parent.

His tiny fists punched the air. Maggie drew him close and held her cheek against his downy head. 'Hush, little one, all is well—you survived. God be praised! Know this, I will always love you. My heart will always hold you close. It is torn in two as I look down upon your beauty. Forgive me, but I cannot burden you with my life. When I next hold you, it will be in Heaven when we are reunited in the afterworld. I cannot let you live in my world on earth. You deserve better, and my husband does not deserve you. He is not your blood, and I cannot bring myself to inflict him upon you.

Your true father will never know you exist. He made his choices in life, as I have to make mine.' Her voice was soft and tender as she crooned the only words she would ever say to her child.

Maggie wiped away the tears and gathered her belongings. The little boy lay in a wicker basket she had woven from soft wood. She had made a quilt in secret, from rags and old clothing casual farm workers had left lying around over the past six months. From the moment she realised her pregnancy, she had prepared for this day. Each item had to be anonymous—there could be no connection to her or the farm.

She tied a rag around her waist and wedged it between her legs to absorb any blood. It chafed as she moved. She was sticky and sore, and the walk across the field to the roadside was a long and painful one. Each bump of the basket tugged her insides. Now was not a good time to stop and adjust the rag for comfort.

Maggie reached the long main road leading into the centre of Redgrave village. It was tree-lined with large horse chestnut and sycamore trees. A russet carpet of leaves lay across the pathways, and the white tower of St Mary's church was to her left. It indicated the south side of the village and marked approximately one mile away from where she stood.

Maggie turned her back to the majestic building and looked to the distance at a lone, large shape on the brow of a hill. Dark and dismal against the powder blue skyline was the outline of her home. It sat central to smaller buildings and appeared forlorn among the furrowed lines of grey, brown fields and dilapidated fencing. The north side; the side that love forgot. It looked every bit as depressing as it was. Even a bright autumn day could not improve the view. A cruel fact of Maggie's world gave her the nudge forward she needed. There was no turning back.

Shaking off the dark mood that threatened, she scouted around for a safe spot in the shade. The midday sun was not fierce, but it could dehydrate an unattended child quickly, especially a new-born. Gently, Maggie placed the basket with its squalling contents on the ground beside a large wall of greenery. The gorse bush would protect him from stray animals and give him shelter but still allow him to be found. Despite the temptation, she did not touch him again. Maggie knew her resolve would break down. It would be so easy to scoop him into her arms and take him home.

Fight it, Maggie! Fight the urge!

Blowing him a kiss to last a lifetime, Maggie walked away with a heavy heart. Regret and remorse had no place inside the gap he had left at the present time. She would grieve later. Prayers—and hope— were her companions. Crawling into a small hollow of a hedge, Maggie lay low between the hawthorn and gorse. Her head ached, and she was thirsty. There were only two hours left before her husband would miss her, and Maggie prayed for a swift remedy to her predicament. It would be easier to walk away, but she wanted to see who claimed the child. She needed to reassure herself that all would be well in his new world. Should an unsavoury passer-by pick him up, she would show herself and pretend she was answering the call of nature. Maggie had spent months contemplating how to secure a safe home for her child. To give birth and walk through the village holding a child was not feasible. To give birth, hide a baby until dark, then place it on the doorstep of someone with money was not possible, either. A plan was needed, and this was the only one Maggie could come up with. Not ideal but necessary.

Her nipples tingled with the urge to feed her child. Her blouse was soaked. She fought against Mother Nature.

Her son screamed for his mother. The louder his cries, the more the first breast fluids flowed, and she resisted with all her might. Brambles scraped at her legs; she crouched low and placed her hands over her ears. Tears ignored her inner battle; they flowed, adding to the dampness of her clothing.

Her insides ached with the need to hold him. To inhale his sweet baby perfume one last time. The want was so powerful! Suddenly she remembered something she had meant to tell him.

'Nathaniel,' she whispered on the wind, 'your name is Nathaniel. I forgot to tell you—forgive me.'

The pain between her legs subsided to a dull throb. The tender belly area was not so uncomfortable, but the pain in her heart would never leave. Temptation was building by the second. If she took him home, she could only enjoy his baby life and protect him for a few years. However, after that, it would be a life of drudgery and aggression. One she had endured since the age of fifteen.

With no consideration for Maggie, her parents had sold her to a widower. A man with no morals or love in his bones. A stray dog showed Maggie more affection with one sniff than Jacob Sawbury had shown her in five years. He lay on top of her and grunted like a pig from the sty in order to reproduce.

If Nathaniel's biological father, Stephen Avenell, knew the truth, he might be tempted to take him from the farm. Their secret would be discovered. If her husband found out the truth, he would destroy all three of them. He would take pride in being the one to bring scandal to the doorstep of the squire. The safest thing to do was to hope someone investigated the wailing sounds. Maggie prayed Nathaniel would not cry himself to sleep.

Keep screaming, my son! I will come for you one day. Dear God, just give me a chance to glimpse who takes him.

She knew she would never take him from whoever gave him a home, but Maggie needed to know where he would spend his years. If she did not recognise his rescuer, she would follow them until she knew where he had been taken. She could make discreet enquiries if he was given a home elsewhere. Locally, it would be easy to trace a new-born.

For fifteen minutes, she listened to the caw-caw of crows, the screams of the child and her heartbeat as it pounded within her chest.

A cart rolled by, and the noise from the wheels against the flint and rocks drowned out the sounds from the basket. Gold-brown leaves fluttered upon the breeze each wheel produced. Maggie watched with trepidation as the driver stopped a few feet away from the area where the babe lay. A large man in working clothes jumped down. He looked around and walked across towards where Maggie crouched.

She shrank back into the hedge. Twigs tangled in her hair and scratched her face. To her horror, it became obvious he was about to relieve himself. He fumbled with the button fly and rummaged around his crotch, freeing his flaccid appendage. She assumed he was desperate to heed the call of nature; it was unbelievable he would simply ignore the cries.

Maggie held her breath as the man urinated. She raised her head a fraction to see if she recognised him. She dared not move too much for fear of distracting him.

Her stomach gave a small flip of disappointment.

Luck was not on her side. The man was Colin Daker, the miller's help. A pleasant man, but he had birth afflictions. He was a deaf-mute. Not one sound would penetrate his eardrums. Nathaniel could scream until he had no air left in his lungs, and Colin still would not respond. Because she had placed the basket in the shade of a bush, Nathaniel would have to cry to be found by Colin. He would never see the child by chance as he was too far away from the bush.

Maggie focused upon Colin, staring at the back of his head as he walked away. She willed him to look to his right and around the bend of the hedge. Hope upon hope was thrown his way in silent, invisible words.

Look, just look down! Move around the corner. He's there—find him, Colin! You are a good man; you will do right by him. Please just look.

'Hey there. You, man, move your cart.'

Maggie was shaken out of her trance-like state and shrunk back into the hedging. A deep, well-spoken voice was responsible. While she had been concentrating upon

Colin, she had not noticed a horse-drawn carriage pull up behind his cart.

Colin, oblivious to the fact that he had been spoken to, waved back in acknowledgement when he saw the driver wave to him. He climbed upon his cart and pulled away. Maggie's heart sank as the carriage moved forward.

'Wait—stop the carriage!' a female voice called out to the driver through the open window.

It was the voice of Felicity Arlington. The woman read Bible verses in church on a regular basis, enough times for Maggie to know who she was.

'Whatever is it, Flick?' the man who had called out to Colin used a pet name, but Maggie knew it was not the voice of Mr Arlington; his was much deeper.

The carriage door opened, and a woman in her late twenties climbed down. Her boots were dainty, tan and, Maggie noted, made of expensive leather. She thought of her own black, shabby ones, in need of another repair, and shook her head. Her feet would never house anything so luxurious.

'Shush. Listen! I can hear a strange noise. Listen!' Mrs Arlington put her fingers to her lips and looked about her.

A young man about the same age clambered down from the carriage and stood beside her, shaking his head.

"tis a kitten. A cat has a litter around somewhere. It is coming from over there.' He pointed towards the gorse bush that housed Nathaniel, he cocked his head to one side, then nodded and put his finger to his lips to silence those around him. He tiptoed slowly towards the noise.

Maggie squeezed her hands together. Her stomach tensed; her son was about to be found. She raised her head and sent another silent prayer to the wind. This time it was to thank God for sending Felicity Arlington. A good woman with a caring soul. Her family was an upstanding, honest one within the Suffolk community. Nathaniel would be safe in their care.

'Goodness—Flick, come here! It is not a kitten, 'tis—well—a baby in a basket! A tiny baby!' The man lifted the basket from the ground and brought it out from under the bush. His face flushed, he hurried towards the carriage.

Maggie sat mesmerised as the woman gently lifted her son from his bed. His fists clenched, and his arms flayed around him. His cries were frantic.

Felicity patted his back and held him close to her chest. All the time, Maggie was crying inside, and more than a twinge of envy passed through her. At least the woman cared for him—she was affectionate and comforted him.

'Oh, you poor little thing! Who has left you here alone? There, there, do not cry, sweet child, we will help.' She turned to the man who was still holding the basket.

'I cannot see anyone around. Get Dukes to see if the mother is lying sick somewhere! This baby isn't many hours old.'

The two men walked in opposite directions, and for several minutes, his mother watched as the woman stood cradling him. A stranger crooned soothing words of comfort.

'Hush now. Who could have done something like this? Who has abandoned you here? How frightened you must be alone. Never you mind, you are not alone now.'

Maggie wanted to run to her and snatch him away. To declare he was not abandoned; she thought about where he had been placed, she wanted him, but she could not keep him. She wanted to explain how he came to be there, but knew it was wise to stay in her hiding place.

'I cannot see anyone around, madam. The man in the cart was Colin Daker.' Dukes, the driver, stood with his hands behind his back and waited for further instructions.

'Dukes, did you see anything? I haven't noticed anyone walking around.' The young man strode up beside the woman.

'Dukes said he has not, and the man on the cart was the deaf-mute from the mill. He would not abandon a child. 'tis obvious he would not have heard it crying. What are you going to do with the baby? He needs attending to. Thanks to our Lord, *we* found him, and not a mangy dog. For I fear he will not last the day without sustenance.'

(End of sample)

If you enjoyed this sample, you can read reviews and purchase the book via these links: [Glynis Smy Novels](#)

Available in Kindle ebook and Paperback format.

Praise for Maggie's Child:

Glynis Smy has created a historical world that puts me in mind of the classic works of George Eliot and Elizabeth Gaskell.
Her hard-working, put-upon heroine carries herself with a quiet grace through the tragedies of her hard-fought life.
Not a cheerful story in many respects (there are moments in which it is quite dark), but the author plumbs the depths of human darkness and comes up in the end with a bucket full of light and hope.
K.M. Weiland, Author of Historical and Speculative Fiction

It is one o'clock in the morning, and I couldn't go to sleep until I had finished reading this latest book by Glynis Smy. It has really captured my imagination with its intriguing plot and colorful characters. The book is a real page-turner and one which I would rank up there with Josephine Cox, Marie Joseph and Anna Jacobs, three of my all-time favorite authors of historical fiction. It gives us a deep insight into the hardships of life in the nineteenth century. The heroine, Maggie, suffers dreadful cruelty at the hands of her miserly husband and through the love of her child, whom she cannot acknowledge she is determined to rise above it, and eventually finds true love. This is a beautifully written book which I can highly recommend. Christine Ramsey – Reader

Printed in Great Britain
by Amazon.co.uk, Ltd.,
Marston Gate.